THE PELICAN SHAKESPEARE

GENERAL EDITOR ALFRED HARBAGE

OTHELLO THE MOOR OF VENICE

WILLIAM SHAKESPEARE

OTHELLO
THE MOOR OF
VENICE

EDITED BY GERALD EADES BENTLEY

PENGUIN BOOKS

PENGUIN BOOKS
Published by the Penguin Group
Penguin Books USA Inc.,
375 Hudson Street, New York, New York 10014, U.S.A.
Penguin Books Ltd, 27 Wrights Lane, London W8 5TZ, England
Penguin Books Australia Ltd, Ringwood,
Victoria, Australia
Penguin Books Canada Ltd, 10 Alcorn Avenue,
Toronto, Ontario, Canada M4V 3B2
Penguin Books (N.Z.) Ltd, 182–190 Wairau Road,
Auckland 10, New Zealand

Penguin Books Ltd, Registered Offices:
Harmondsworth, Middlesex, England

First published in *The Pelican Shakespeare* 1958
This revised edition first published 1970

27   29   30   28   26

Library of Congress catalog card number: 71-98371

ISBN 0 14 071410 3

Printed in the United States of America
Set in Monotype Ehrhardt

CONTENTS

PUBLISHER'S NOTE

Soon after the thirty-eight volumes forming *The Pelican Shakespeare* had been published, they were brought together in *The Complete Pelican Shakespeare*. The editorial revisions and new textual features are explained in detail in the General Editor's Preface to the one-volume edition. They have all been incorporated in the present volume. The following should be mentioned in particular:

The lines are not numbered in arbitrary units. Instead all lines are numbered which contain a word, phrase, or allusion explained in the glossarial notes. In the occasional instances where there is a long stretch of unannotated text, certain lines are numbered in italics to serve the conventional reference purpose.

The intrusive and often inaccurate place-headings inserted by early editors are omitted (as is becoming standard practise), but for the convenience of those who miss them, an indication of locale now appears as first item in the annotation of each scene.

In the interest of both elegance and utility, each speech-prefix is set in a separate line when the speaker's lines are in verse, except when these words form the second half of a pentameter line. Thus the verse form of the speech is kept visually intact, and turned-over lines are avoided. What is printed as verse and what is printed as prose has, in general, the authority of the original texts. Departures from the original texts in this regard have only the authority of editorial tradition and the judgment of the Pelican editors; and, in a few instances, are admittedly arbitrary.

SHAKESPEARE AND
HIS STAGE

William Shakespeare was christened in Holy Trinity
Church, Stratford-upon-Avon, April 26, 1564. His birth
is traditionally assigned to April 23. He was the eldest of
four boys and two girls who survived infancy in the family
of John Shakespeare, glover and trader of Henley Street,
and his wife Mary Arden, daughter of a small landowner
of Wilmcote. In 1568 John was elected Bailiff (equivalent
to Mayor) of Stratford, having already filled the minor
municipal offices. The town maintained for the sons of the
burgesses a free school, taught by a university graduate
and offering preparation in Latin sufficient for university
entrance; its early registers are lost, but there can be little
doubt that Shakespeare received the formal part of his
education in this school.

On November 27, 1582, a license was issued for the
marriage of William Shakespeare (aged eighteen) and Ann
Hathaway (aged twenty-six), and on May 26, 1583, their
child Susanna was christened in Holy Trinity Church.
The inference that the marriage was forced upon the youth
is natural but not inevitable; betrothal was legally binding
at the time, and was sometimes regarded as conferring
conjugal rights. Two additional children of the marriage,
the twins Hamnet and Judith, were christened on Feb-
ruary 2, 1585. Meanwhile the prosperity of the elder
Shakespeares had declined, and William was impelled to
seek a career outside Stratford.

The tradition that he spent some time as a country

teacher is old but unverifiable. Because of the absence of records his early twenties are called the "lost years," and only one thing about them is certain – that at least some of these years were spent in winning a place in the acting profession. He may have begun as a provincial trouper, but by 1592 he was established in London and prominent enough to be attacked. In a pamphlet of that year, *Groats-worth of Wit*, the ailing Robert Greene complained of the neglect which university writers like himself had suffered from actors, one of whom was daring to set up as a playwright:

... an vpstart Crow, beautified with our feathers, that with his *Tygers hart wrapt in a Players hyde*, supposes he is as well able to bombast out a blanke verse as the best of you: and beeing an absolute *Iohannes fac totum*, is in his owne conceit the onely Shake-scene in a countrey.

The pun on his name, and the parody of his line "O tiger's heart wrapped in a woman's hide" (*3 Henry VI*), pointed clearly to Shakespeare. Some of his admirers protested, and Henry Chettle, the editor of Greene's pamphlet, saw fit to apologize:

... I am as sory as if the originall fault had beene my fault, because my selfe haue seene his demeanor no lesse ciuill than he excelent in the qualitie he professes: Besides, diuers of worship haue reported his vprightnes of dealing, which argues his honesty, and his faceti-ous grace in writting, that approoues his Art. (Prefatory epistle, *Kind-Harts Dreame*)

The plague closed the London theatres for many months in 1592–94, denying the actors their livelihood. To this period belong Shakespeare's two narrative poems, *Venus and Adonis* and *The Rape of Lucrece*, both dedicated to the Earl of Southampton. No doubt the poet was rewarded with a gift of money as usual in such cases, but he did no further dedicating and we have no reliable information on whether Southampton, or anyone else, became his regular patron. His sonnets, first mentioned in 1598 and published without his consent in 1609, are intimate without being explicitly autobiographical. They seem to commemorate the poet's friendship with an idealized youth, rivalry with a more favored poet, and love affair with a dark mistress; and his bitterness when the mistress betrays him in conjunction with the friend; but it is difficult to decide precisely what the "story" is, impossible to decide whether it is fictional or true. The true distinction of the sonnets, at least of those not purely conventional, rests in the universality of the thoughts and moods they express, and in their poignancy and beauty.

In 1594 was formed the theatrical company known until 1603 as the Lord Chamberlain's men, thereafter as the King's men. Its original membership included, besides Shakespeare, the beloved clown Will Kempe and the famous actor Richard Burbage. The company acted in various London theatres and even toured the provinces, but it is chiefly associated in our minds with the Globe Theatre built on the south bank of the Thames in 1599. Shakespeare was an actor and joint owner of this company (and its Globe) through the remainder of his creative years. His plays, written at the average rate of two a year, together with Burbage's acting won it its place of leadership among the London companies.

Individual plays began to appear in print, in editions both honest and piratical, and the publishers became increasingly aware of the value of Shakespeare's name on the title pages. As early as 1598 he was hailed as the leading English dramatist in the *Palladis Tamia* of Francis Meres:

As *Plautus* and *Seneca* are accounted the best for Comedy and Tragedy among the Latines, so *Shakespeare* among the English is the most excellent in both kinds for the stage: for Comedy, witnes his *Gentlemen of Verona*, his *Errors*, his *Loue labors lost*, his *Loue labours wonne* [at one time in print but no longer extant, at least under this title], his *Midsummers night dream*, & his *Merchant of Venice*; for Tragedy, his *Richard the 2*, *Richard the 3*, *Henry the 4*, *King Iohn*, *Titus Andronicus*, and his *Romeo and Iuliet*.

The note is valuable both in indicating Shakespeare's prestige and in helping us to establish a chronology. In the second half of his writing career, history plays gave place to the great tragedies; and farces and light comedies gave place to the problem plays and symbolic romances. In 1623, seven years after his death, his former fellow-actors, John Heminge and Henry Condell, cooperated with a group of London printers in bringing out his plays in collected form. The volume is generally known as the First Folio.

Shakespeare had never severed his relations with Stratford. His wife and children may sometimes have shared his London lodgings, but their home was Stratford. His son Hamnet was buried there in 1596, and his daughters Susanna and Judith were married there in 1607 and 1616 respectively. (His father, for whom he had secured a coat of arms and thus the privilege of writing himself gentleman, died in 1601, his mother in 1608.) His considerable earnings in London, as actor-sharer, part owner of the Globe, and playwright, were invested chiefly in Stratford property. In 1597 he purchased for £60 New Place, one of the two most imposing residences in the town. A number of other business transactions, as well as minor episodes in his career, have left documentary records. By 1611 he was in a position to retire, and he seems gradually to have withdrawn from theatrical activity in order to live in Stratford. In March, 1616, he made a will, leaving token bequests to Burbage, Heminge, and Condell, but the bulk of his estate to his family. The most famous feature of the will, the bequest of the second-best bed to his wife, reveals nothing about Shakespeare's marriage; the quaintness of the provision seems commonplace to those familiar with ancient testaments. Shakespeare died April 23, 1616, and was buried in the Stratford church where he had been christened. Within seven years a monument was erected to his memory on the north wall of the chancel. Its portrait bust and the Droeshout engraving on the title page of the First Folio provide the only likenesses with an established claim to authenticity. The best verbal vignette was written by his rival Ben Jonson, the more impressive for being imbedded in a context mainly critical:

. . . I loved the man, and doe honour his memory (on this side idolatry) as much as any. Hee was indeed honest, and of an open and free nature: had an excellent Phantsie, brave notions, and gentle expressions. . . . (*Timber or Discoveries*, ca. 1623–30)

*

The reader of Shakespeare's plays is aided by a general knowledge of the way in which they were staged. The King's men acquired a roofed and artificially lighted theatre only toward the close of Shakespeare's career, and then only for winter use. Nearly all his plays were designed for performance in such structures as the Globe – a three-tiered amphitheatre with a large rectangular platform extending to the center of its yard. The plays were staged by daylight, by large casts brilliantly costumed, but with only a minimum of properties, without scenery, and quite possibly without intermissions. There was a rear stage gallery for action "above," and a curtained rear recess for "discoveries" and other special effects, but by far the major portion of any play was enacted upon the projecting platform, with episode following episode in swift succession, and with shifts of time and place signaled the audience only by the momentary clearing of the stage between the episodes. Information about the identity of the characters and, when necessary, about the time and place of the action was incorporated in the dialogue. No place-headings have been inserted in the present editions; these are apt to obscure the original fluidity of structure, with the emphasis upon action and speech rather than scenic background. (Indications of place are supplied in the footnotes.) The acting, including that of the youthful apprentices to the profession who performed the parts of women, was highly skillful, with a premium placed upon grace of gesture and beauty of diction. The audiences, a cross section of the general public, commonly numbered a thousand, sometimes more than two thousand. Judged by the type of plays they applauded, these audiences were not only large but also perceptive.

THE TEXTS OF THE PLAYS

About half of Shakespeare's plays appeared in print for the first time in the folio volume of 1623. The others had been published individually, usually in quarto volumes, during his lifetime or in the six years following his death. The copy used by the printers of the quartos varied greatly in merit, sometimes representing Shakespeare's true text, sometimes only a debased version of that text. The copy used by the printers of the folio also varied in merit, but was chosen with care. Since it consisted of the best available manuscripts, or the more acceptable quartos (although frequently in editions other than the first), or of quartos corrected by reference to manuscripts, we have good or reasonably good texts of most of the thirty-seven plays.

In the present series, the plays have been newly edited from quarto or folio texts, depending, when a choice offered, upon which is now regarded by bibliographical specialists as the more authoritative. The ideal has been to reproduce the chosen texts with as few alterations as possible, beyond occasional relineation, expansion of abbreviations, and modernization of punctuation and spelling. Emendation is held to a minimum, and such material as has been added, in the way of stage directions and lines supplied by an alternative text, has been enclosed in square brackets.

None of the plays printed in Shakespeare's lifetime were divided into acts and scenes, and the inference is that the author's own manuscripts were not so divided. In the folio collection, some of the plays remained undivided, some were divided into acts, and some were divided into acts and scenes. During the eighteenth century all of the plays were divided into acts and scenes, and in the Cambridge edition of the mid-nineteenth century, from which the influential Globe text derived, this division was more or less regularized and the lines were numbered. Many useful works of reference employ the act–scene–line apparatus thus established.

Since this act–scene division is obviously convenient, but is of very dubious authority so far as Shakespeare's own structural principles are concerned, or the original manner of staging his plays, a problem is presented to modern editors. In the present series the act–scene division is retained marginally, and may be viewed as a reference aid like the line numbering. A star marks the points of division when these points have been determined by a cleared stage indicating a shift of time and place in the action of the play, or when no harm results from the editorial assumption that there is such a shift. However, at those points where the established division is clearly misleading – that is, where continuous action has been split up into separate "scenes" – the star is omitted and the distortion corrected. This mechanical expedient seemed the best means of combining utility and accuracy.

THE GENERAL EDITOR

INTRODUCTION

Of the four tragedies commonly thought to be Shakespeare's greatest and the most distinguished examples of this form in the English language – *Hamlet*, *Othello*, *King Lear*, and *Macbeth* – *Othello* is the most tightly constructed and the narrowest in scope. The resultant concentration of emotion and action makes it a play of unusual forcefulness, powerful not only on the stage but in the study, sweeping from the confident and brilliant opening to the tragic close. All four tragedies came within a six- or seven-year span; *Othello*, the second, was probably written not long before November 1, 1604, when it was performed by the King's Men at Court, and it is interesting that it alone has this tight construction and headlong action.

Shakespeare gains this concentration in several ways. For one thing, here the time of action is condensed so that the events of only two or three nights and days appear to be set forth on the stage, and the only emphasized time-lapse is that required for the voyage from Venice to Cyprus. The other three tragedies span months or even years, and time-consuming events which occur between scenes have to be pointed out to the audience: for example, in *Hamlet* Laertes' trip from Elsinore to Paris and return; in *King Lear* Cordelia's sojourn in France; and in *Macbeth* Malcolm and Macduff's flight to England, the recruitment of an army there, and then the march of that army to Dunsinane. The elimination in *Othello* of all but one such emphasized space-breaks and time-breaks helps to give the play its headlong rush from the arrival in Cyprus to Othello's death.

Not only by a limitation of time has Shakespeare intensified the effect of rushing events, but also by an unusual concentration of the action in the three main characters, Othello, Desdemona, and Iago. One or more of these three is on the stage in each of the fifteen scenes of the play except for the brief proclamation scene (II, ii), whereas Macbeth and Lady Macbeth are absent from nine scenes of their play, Lear and his daughters fail to appear in six scenes of *King Lear*, and even in the one-man play of *Hamlet* both the protagonist and Ophelia are off-stage during four scenes totalling nearly five hundred lines. These observations afford, of course, no evidence of the comparative merits of the four tragedies, but they do point to Shakespeare's deviation from his customary practice in achieving the distinctive concentration of *Othello*. He has denied himself the development of any subsidiary interests in order to concentrate on the tragic destruction of Othello and Desdemona through the diabolism of Iago.

To the same end Shakespeare has minimized the number of characters in this play. Not only is the cast of *Othello* smaller than those of the other three tragedies – it has half to two-thirds the number of characters – but in it the secondary characters, Brabantio, Cassio, Roderigo, and Emilia, are undeveloped save for their relations to the plotting of Iago or the downfall of Othello and Desdemona. Even Iago's gulling of Roderigo, which might at first glance seem to be an underplot, is really only an instrument in the destruction of Othello ; Roderigo is given little individuality beyond that of the uncomprehending gull to whom Iago may speak freely (thus further revealing for the audience his own character and plans) and who will carry out Iago's schemes for the disgrace and assassination of Cassio. Roderigo has no unrelated or parallel existence, like that of Lady Macduff in *Macbeth*, or Polonius and Fortinbras in *Hamlet*. All such secondary concerns, which add variety and depth of character-interest to Shakespeare's other major tragedies, and to *Romeo and Juliet*, *Julius Caesar*, *Antony and Cleopatra*, and *Coriolanus* as well, have been sacrificed in this play to give *Othello* that unique concentration and simplicity which make it more like modern tragedies in structure than any of Shakespeare's other tragic masterpieces.

Othello differs again from the usual Shakespearean pattern in the extent to which the power of evil is concentrated in one figure. The conflict of good and evil in an ostensibly Christian world was always a basic element in Elizabethan tragedies, and Shakespeare's presentation of the conflict is everywhere more subtle and complex than that of any of his contemporaries, but in the other Shakespearean tragedies the evil is more dispersed through various characters or even, as in *King Lear*, through the entire world of the play. Here the inherent weaknesses of Desdemona and Othello are made fatal through the maneuvering of Iago, whose cunning of the devil makes the finally disabused Othello look for his cloven hoof (V, ii, 286). This further simplification of the structure of the play not only makes possible the creation of Shakespeare's supreme stage villain – one of the most coveted roles in the history of the theatre – but it provides yet another device for the concentration of emotions in the tragedy. The play's excellence in structure and vividness in characterization seem even more impressive when *Othello* is compared with its source, a mediocre Italian tale by "Cinthio" (Giovanni Baptista Giraldi) told in the *Hecatommithi*, a collection of 1565.

Having planned his scenario to reduce the scope and variety made possible by the Elizabethan stage and familiarly exploited in tragedies like his own *Antony and Cleopatra* and Marlowe's *Doctor Faustus*, Shakespeare could lavish his dramatic and poetic genius on the painful degen-

eration of the noble and assured Othello of Act I, scenes
ii and iii, to the pitiful dupe and the figure of passionate
remorse we see in V, ii; on the battering of the proud and
confident Desdemona of I, iii into the childlike and uncomprehending victim of Acts IV and V – all by means of
the terrifyingly casual and joyous evil of "honest Iago."
All the seeds of these tragic events are displayed to the
audience in the first act, but they are so adroitly overlaid
by a romantic and optimistic tone that the prosperity of
the love of Othello and Desdemona is made to seem
superficially possible.

Othello is a man of action whose achievement was immediately obvious to an Elizabethan audience, in spite of
his exotic color and background, because of his position as
the commanding general for the greatest commercial
power of the preceding century. He is first presented in a
situation in which his experience and reputation make him
easily the dominant figure on the stage. In the second
scene of the play, as the drawn swords flash about him,
Othello, the object of the attack, stands quietly confident,
his weapon still in its scabbard, and speaks to these in-
censed men like a veteran to excited boys : "Keep up your
bright swords, for the dew will rust them."

At Othello's second appearance, in the third scene of
the play, he dominates not a mere cluster of street fighters
but the Duke and senators of a powerful Renaissance state
assembled in formal council. The scene is skillfully contrived at the beginning to draw the audience into the crisis
of a national emergency; then a principal senator arrives
who focuses the attention of the council on his just
indignation against the unnamed seducer of his daughter.
Unhesitatingly the Duke accepts Brabantio's story and
unhesitatingly promises him the bloody punishment of
the culprit, though the man be the Duke's own son. But
when Brabantio explains that the unnamed seducer is
their great general, the attitude of Duke and senators
changes sharply. Respectfully they listen as the black

Othello describes his courtship of the daughter of a great
Venetian magnifico; they watch sympathetically as Desdemona confesses her duty and obedience to the Moor
above her duty and obedience to her father; the Duke in
the presence of the other senators advises Brabantio to
make the best of his new son-in-law; and Duke and
senators proceed to reiterate their confidence in Othello
by assigning him the command at Cyprus as though Brabantio had never spoken. Again, as in scene ii, the assured
power of Othello over great men in council as well as over
lesser men in action is dramatized before the audience.

Yet under this dominating impression of a commanding
and unshakeable personality the weaknesses of Othello have
been less vividly suggested. In the second scene he speaks
confidentially to Iago as to a trusted friend, and toward
the end of the third scene he commits his beloved wife to
the protection of Iago, whom he calls a man "of honesty
and trust." But the audience had been introduced to Iago
before they had been to Othello. In the opening scene of
the play Iago was heard to admit his hatred of Othello, to
declare his moral code as unscrupulous self-aggrandize-
ment, and to assert his policy of consistent insincerity.
And in the council chamber scene, immediately after the
exit of Othello, the trusted Iago again declares his principles of calculated self-seeking and closes the act with a
soliloquy in which he reasserts his hatred of Othello and
plots the general's betrayal. Can Othello's assured mastery
of threatening situations be so unshakeable as it has seemed
in the two big dramatic scenes of the act if he is so naive in
his judgment of Iago?

And what of the romantic marriage with Desdemona so
touchingly presented? Othello says of his wife that

> She loved me for the dangers I had passed,
> And I loved her that she did pity them.

The lines are beautifully evocative, but many members of
the audience might have an uneasy feeling that Desde-

mona really knew very little about Othello. And they would feel uneasy again at Brabantio's bitter parting jibe at Othello,

> Look to her, Moor, if thou hast eyes to see:
> She has deceived her father, and may thee,

a jibe made in a spirit of animosity and not of thoughtful analysis, yet reminding us that romantic ignorance often prepares the way for deception. The Elizabethan ideal of respect for parents was much stronger than ours, and this emphatic couplet was calculated to make a sharper impression on an audience than a more elaborately rational statement would have made. Even the phrase "if thou hast eyes to see" has an ominous relevance, for Othello has already shown he has no eyes to see the true character of Iago. Does he know more of Desdemona?

And so carefully planned concentration on Iago, Othello, and Desdemona in the first act of the play leaves a dominant impression of a resourceful and confident general, triumphant in a seriously threatened love affair, off for new triumphs in the field of his greatest competence, so fortunate that as he sets out to meet the challenge of a military emergency he is not even required to forgo the company of his bride. And yet here, less dominantly presented in this opening movement, are all the seeds of the fifth act. Othello is a proud and confident man, but his experience, as he himself points out, is almost exclusively military; his appealing new wife knows little of him save for his military honors and adventures, and he knows little of her save for her admiration of his exploits; his trusted ensign is an unscrupulous opportunist who prides himself on his insincerity. In these terms the play is to develop.

The transfer of the action to Cyprus for the developments of the last four acts is significant. From Desdemona's native world of wealthy, sophisticated, pampered Venice, where Othello is out of his usual campaign environment, the action moves to an outpost under martial law, a setting alien to Desdemona. Here, like most of Shakespeare's tragic heroines, she is isolated from her accustomed friends and supporters, while Othello is in a setting familiar, as he has said, from childhood :

> For since these arms of mine had seven years' pith
> Till now some nine moons wasted, they have used
> Their dearest action in the tented field.

In such an environment one would expect Othello to be even more effortlessly dominant than in worldly Venice, and the first two hundred lines of the Cyprus action suggest that he will be, for all on stage are relieved at his arrival and eager to trust and serve him ; even the fortunate dispersal of the Turkish fleet seems another triumph for lucky Othello. But it only seems so, for Othello's accustomed environment of war is suddenly removed, and in the last hundred lines of II, i Iago establishes the cynical, lecherous, intriguing tone of a decadent Renaissance court more vividly than it was ever set in the first act at Venice itself. Othello's apparent good fortune in the transfer of the action from sophisticated Venice, where, as he says, "little of this great world can I speak," to the familiar setting of a town at war, with the added good fortune of the company of his bride, is a completely illusory triumph. Cyprus is not really an honest camp but an outpost of Venetian intrigue in which Othello is a helpless child ; his new wife is not even a typical Venetian, for she is more naive and imperceptive than Othello, as her actions in the third and fourth acts and her conversation with Emilia in the last part of IV, iii so vividly show ; Iago is not the trusty ensign who will fight at his commander's side but a Venetian devil incarnate, adept at hellish insinuations. As in so many Shakespearean tragedies, the great man of the first act enters a new set of circumstances and becomes "no more but such a poor, bare, forked animal as thou art."

It is only Iago who prospers in the new environment.

The declared villain satisfies his hatred of his general and his lieutenant by creating for Othello the vivid illusion of Desdemona's infidelity with Cassio, and in the terrifying grip of this illusion Othello destroys his reputation, his happiness, his bride, and himself. Perhaps the most tragically terrifying aspect of this irrational destruction is the fact that Othello, like all mortals who only know in part, dimly realizes what he is doing at each step, but in the grip of the illusion he always misunderstands why he is doing it. As early as the middle of the third act he knows that his suspicious uncertainty of Desdemona has destroyed his peace of mind and his cherished professional career.

> O, now for ever
> Farewell the tranquil mind ! farewell content !
> Farewell the plumèd troop, and the big wars
> That make ambition virtue ! O, farewell !
> Farewell the neighing steed and the shrill trump,
> The spirit-stirring drum, th' ear-piercing fife,
> The royal banner, and all quality,
> Pride, pomp, and circumstance of glorious war !
> And O you mortal engines whose rude throats
> Th' immortal Jove's dread clamors counterfeit,
> Farewell ! Othello's occupation's gone !

When he comes in to kill Desdemona he is painfully aware that his love for her is as deep as ever, that he destroys what he loves best. He kisses the sleeping girl.

> O balmy breath, that dost almost persuade
> Justice to break her sword ! One more, one more !
> Be thus when thou art dead, and I will kill thee,
> And love thee after. One more, and that's the last !
> So sweet was ne'er so fatal. I must weep,
> But they are cruel tears. This sorrow's heavenly ;
> It strikes where it doth love.

And a few lines later when she protests her innocence he partially and confusedly understands what he does :

> O perjured woman ! thou dost stone my heart,
> And mak'st me call what I intend to do
> A murder, which I thought a sacrifice.

When, immediately after the stifling of Desdemona,
Emilia enters the death chamber with news of the street
murder, Othello again vaguely recognizes what he has
done in the madness of his illusion, though he speaks in
general terms :

> It is the very error of the moon.
> She comes more nearer earth than she was wont
> And makes men mad.

And when Emilia roundly asserts the fidelity of her dead
mistress, Othello protests in half-realization of his illusion,

> Cassio did top her. Ask thy husband else.
> O, I were damned beneath all depth in hell
> But that I did proceed upon just grounds
> To this extremity. Thy husband knew it all.

Only in the last hundred lines of the play does he clearly
begin to see himself and to comprehend what has hap-
pened to him :

> with this little arm and this good sword
> I have made my way through more impediments
> Than twenty times your stop. But O vain boast !
> Who can control his fate ? 'Tis not so now.
> Be not afraid, though you do see me weaponed.
> Here is my journey's end.

And only in his final speech to the emissaries from the
Duke and senators, just before he stabs himself, does the
great general of Venice, like the great King Lear, truly
know himself :

> I pray you, in your letters,
> When you shall these unlucky deeds relate,
> Speak of me as I am. Nothing extenuate,
> Nor set down aught in malice. Then must you speak

Of one that loved not wisely, but too well;
Of one not easily jealous, but, being wrought,
Perplexed in the extreme; of one whose hand,
Like the base Judean, threw a pearl away
Richer than all his tribe.

This is the tragedy, then, of another deluded mortal who destroys what he loves best, so that his own death is only an appropriate corollary. King Lear and Coriolanus and Brutus do likewise, but they destroy themselves in a context of troubled kingdoms and empires, while the little world of Othello's tragedy is his own marriage and his false friend, "honest Iago." This narrowed scope of the tragedy reduces the generalized philosophic comments which characterize plays of more varied situation and looser structure like *King Lear* and *Hamlet*, but it intensifies the emotional impact of blind self-destruction.

Princeton University   GERALD EADES BENTLEY

NOTE ON THE TEXT

Two versions of *Othello* have come down to us, one in a quarto of 1622 and another in the folio of 1623. Both are good, although they vary somewhat in details and their precise relationship is still subject to debate. The folio version is the fuller (by about 160 lines) and has been used as the basis of the present text; however, a number of readings from the quarto have been admitted, especially in contractions, oaths, and stage directions, where the corresponding words in the folio suggest editorial intervention. A few lines and brief passages of dialogue (I, iii, 372–75; III, iv, 92–93) omitted from the folio have been added from the quarto in square brackets. The act–scene division supplied marginally for reference is identical with that of the folio except for the indication of a new scene (II, iii) after the reading of the proclamation. (Unlike earlier quartos, that of *Othello* is partially divided into acts, with headings at II, IV, and V.) The extent of the use made of the quarto text is indicated in the Appendix as well as a listing of emendations.

OTHELLO
THE MOOR OF
VENICE

THE NAMES OF THE ACTORS

Othello, the Moor
Brabantio, [a Venetian senator,] father to Desdemona
Cassio, an honorable lieutenant [to Othello]
Iago, [Othello's ancient,] a villain
Roderigo, a gulled gentleman
Duke of Venice
Senators [of Venice]
Montano, governor of Cyprus
Lodovico and Gratiano, [kinsmen to Brabantio,] two noble
  Venetians
Sailors
Clown
Desdemona, wife to Othello
Emilia, wife to Iago
Bianca, a courtesan
[Messenger, Herald, Officers, Venetian Gentlemen,
  Musicians, Attendants

Scene : *Venice and Cyprus]*

OTHELLO
THE MOOR OF
VENICE

Enter Roderigo and Iago.

RODERIGO
  Tush, never tell me! I take it much unkindly
  That thou, Iago, who hast had my purse
  As if the strings were thine, shouldst know of this.   3

IAGO
  'Sblood, but you'll not hear me!   4
  If ever I did dream of such a matter,
  Abhor me.

RODERIGO
  Thou told'st me thou didst hold him in thy hate.

IAGO
  Despise me if I do not. Three great ones of the city,
  In personal suit to make me his lieutenant,
  Off-capped to him; and, by the faith of man,   10
  I know my price; I am worth no worse a place.
  But he, as loving his own pride and purposes,
  Evades them with a bombast circumstance.   13
  Horribly stuffed with epithets of war;
  [And, in conclusion,]
  Nonsuits my mediators; for, 'Certes,' says he,   16
  'I have already chose my officer.'
  And what was he?
  Forsooth, a great arithmetician,   19

---

¹**I, i** A street in Venice   **3** *this* i.e. Desdemona's elopement   **4** *'Sblood* by
God's blood   **10** *him* i.e. Othello   **13** *a bombast circumstance* pompous
circumlocutions   **16** *Nonsuits* rejects   **19** *arithmetician* theoretician

One Michael Cassio, a Florentine
21 (A fellow almost damned in a fair wife)
That never set a squadron in the field,
Nor the division of a battle knows
More than a spinster; unless the bookish theoric,
Wherein the togèd consuls can propose
As masterly as he. Mere prattle without practice
Is all his soldiership. But he, sir, had th' election;
And I (of whom his eyes had seen the proof
At Rhodes, at Cyprus, and on other grounds
30 Christian and heathen) must be belee'd and calmed
31 By debitor and creditor; this counter-caster,
He, in good time, must his lieutenant be,
33 And I – God bless the mark! – his Moorship's ancient.

RODERIGO
By heaven, I rather would have been his hangman.

IAGO
Why, there's no remedy; 'tis the curse of service.
36 Preferment goes by letter and affection,
And not by old gradation, where each second
Stood heir to th' first. Now, sir, be judge yourself,
39 Whether I in any just term am affined
To love the Moor.

RODERIGO   I would not follow him then.

IAGO
O, sir, content you;
I follow him to serve my turn upon him.
We cannot all be masters, nor all masters
Cannot be truly followed. You shall mark
Many a duteous and knee-crooking knave
That, doting on his own obsequious bondage,
Wears out his time, much like his master's ass,
48 For naught but provender; and when he's old, cashiered.

21 *almost . . . wife* (an obscure allusion; Cassio is unmarried, but see IV, i, 123) 30 *belee'd and calmed* left in the lurch 31 *counter-caster* book-keeper 33 *ancient* ensign 36 *affection* favoritism 39 *affined* obliged 48 *cashiered* turned off

Whip me such honest knaves! Others there are
Who, trimmed in forms and visages of duty,   50
Keep yet their hearts attending on themselves;
And, throwing but shows of service on their lords,
Do well thrive by them, and when they have lined their
    coats,
Do themselves homage. These fellows have some soul;
And such a one do I profess myself. For, sir,
It is as sure as you are Roderigo,
Were I the Moor, I would not be Iago.
In following him, I follow but myself;
Heaven is my judge, not I for love and duty,
But seeming so, for my peculiar end;
For when my outward action doth demonstrate
The native act and figure of my heart   62
In compliment extern, 'tis not long after   63
But I will wear my heart upon my sleeve
For daws to peck at; I am not what I am.

RODERIGO
What a full fortune does the thick-lips owe   66
If he can carry't thus!

IAGO   Call up her father,
Rouse him. Make after him, poison his delight,
Proclaim him in the streets. Incense her kinsmen,
And though he in a fertile climate dwell,
Plague him with flies; though that his joy be joy,
Yet throw such changes of vexation on't
As it may lose some color.

RODERIGO
Here is her father's house. I'll call aloud.

IAGO
Do, with like timorous accent and dire yell   75
As when, by night and negligence, the fire

50 *trimmed* dressed up   62 *The . . . heart* what I really believe and intend
63 *compliment extern* outward appearance   66 *thick-lips* (Elizabethans made
no clear distinction between Moors and Negroes); *owe* own   75 *timorous*
terrifying

Is spied in populous cities.

RODERIGO

What, ho, Brabantio ! Signior Brabantio, ho !

IAGO

Awake ! What, ho, Brabantio ! Thieves ! thieves ! thieves !
Look to your house, your daughter, and your bags !
81   Thieves ! thieves !

Brabantio at a window.

BRABANTIO *(above)*

What is the reason of this terrible summons ?
What is the matter there ?

RODERIGO

Signior, is all your family within ?

IAGO

Are your doors locked ?

BRABANTIO   Why, wherefore ask you this ?

IAGO

Zounds, sir, y' are robbed ! For shame, put on your
    gown !
Your heart is burst ; you have lost half your soul.
Even now, now, very now, an old black ram
Is tupping your white ewe. Arise, arise !
90   Awake the snorting citizens with the bell,
Or else the devil will make a grandsire of you.
Arise, I say !

BRABANTIO   What, have you lost your wits ?

RODERIGO

Most reverend signior, do you know my voice ?

BRABANTIO

Not I. What are you ?

RODERIGO

My name is Roderigo.

BRABANTIO   The worser welcome !
I have charged thee not to haunt about my doors.
In honest plainness thou hast heard me say

---

81 s.d. *Brabantio at a window* (added from quarto)   **90** *snorting* snoring

My daughter is not for thee; and now, in madness,
Being full of supper and distemp'ring draughts,
Upon malicious knavery dost thou come
To start my quiet.

RODERIGO
Sir, sir, sir –

BRABANTIO   But thou must needs be sure
My spirit and my place have in them power
To make this bitter to thee.

RODERIGO   Patience, good sir.

BRABANTIO
What tell'st thou me of robbing? This is Venice;
My house is not a grange.   106

RODERIGO   Most grave Brabantio,
In simple and pure soul I come to you.

IAGO Zounds, sir, you are one of those that will not serve
God if the devil bid you. Because we come to do you
service, and you think we are ruffians, you'll have your
daughter covered with a Barbary horse; you'll have
your nephews neigh to you; you'll have coursers for 112
cousins, and gennets for germans.   113

BRABANTIO
What profane wretch art thou?

IAGO I am one, sir, that comes to tell you your daughter
and the Moor are now making the beast with two backs.

BRABANTIO
Thou art a villain.

IAGO   You are – a senator.

BRABANTIO
This thou shalt answer. I know thee, Roderigo.

RODERIGO
Sir, I will answer anything. But I beseech you,
If't be your pleasure and most wise consent,
As partly I find it is, that your fair daughter,

---

106 *grange* isolated farmhouse   112 *nephews* i.e. grandsons   113 *gennets for germans* Spanish horses for near kinsmen

122   At this odd-even and dull watch o' th' night,
      Transported, with no worse nor better guard
      But with a knave of common hire, a gondolier,
      To the gross clasps of a lascivious Moor –
126   If this be known to you, and your allowance,
      We then have done you bold and saucy wrongs;
      But if you know not this, my manners tell me
      We have your wrong rebuke. Do not believe
130   That, from the sense of all civility,
      I thus would play and trifle with your reverence.
      Your daughter, if you have not given her leave,
      I say again, hath made a gross revolt,
      Tying her duty, beauty, wit, and fortunes
135   In an extravagant and wheeling stranger
      Of here and everywhere. Straight satisfy yourself.
      If she be in her chamber, or your house,
      Let loose on me the justice of the state
      For thus deluding you.
      BRABANTIO   Strike on the tinder, ho!
      Give me a taper! Call up all my people!
141   This accident is not unlike my dream.
      Belief of it oppresses me already.
      Light, I say! light!   *Exit [above].*
      IAGO   Farewell, for I must leave you.
      It seems not meet, nor wholesome to my place,
      To be produced – as, if I stay, I shall –
      Against the Moor. For I do know the state,
147   However this may gall him with some check,
148   Cannot with safety cast him; for he's embarked
      With such loud reason to the Cyprus wars,
150   Which even now stand in act, that for their souls
151   Another of his fathom they have none
      To lead their business; in which regard,

122 *odd-even* between night and morning   126 *allowance* approval   130
from the sense in violation   135 *extravagant and wheeling* expatriate and
roving   141 *accident* occurrence   147 *check* reprimand   148 *cast* discharge
150 *stand in act* are going on   151 *fathom* capacity

Though I do hate him as I do hell-pains,
Yet, for necessity of present life,
I must show out a flag and sign of love,
Which is indeed but sign. That you shall surely find him,
Lead to the Sagittary the raisèd search;   157
And there will I be with him. So farewell.   *Exit.* 158
      Enter [below] Brabantio in his nightgown, and
      Servants with torches.

BRABANTIO
It is too true an evil. Gone she is;
And what's to come of my despisèd time
Is naught but bitterness. Now, Roderigo,
Where didst thou see her? – O unhappy girl! –
With the Moor, say'st thou? – Who would be a father? –
How didst thou know 'twas she? – O, she deceives me
Past thought! – What said she to you? – Get moe tapers! 165
Raise all my kindred! – Are they married, think you?

RODERIGO
Truly I think they are.

BRABANTIO
O heaven! How got she out? O treason of the blood!
Fathers, from hence trust not your daughters' minds
By what you see them act. Is there not charms
By which the property of youth and maidhood   171
May be abused? Have you not read, Roderigo,
Of some such thing?

RODERIGO   Yes, sir, I have indeed.

BRABANTIO
Call up my brother. – O, would you had had her! –
Some one way, some another. – Do you know
Where we may apprehend her and the Moor?

RODERIGO
I think I can discover him, if you please
To get good guard and go along with me.

157 *Sagittary* an inn   158 s.d. *nightgown* dressing gown   165 *moe* more
171 *property* nature

33

BRABANTIO

 Pray you lead on. At every house I'll call;
 I may command at most. – Get weapons, ho!
 And raise some special officers of night. –
182 On, good Roderigo; I'll deserve your pains. *Exeunt*.

*

I, ii   *Enter Othello, Iago, and Attendants with torches*.

 IAGO

 Though in the trade of war I have slain men,
 Yet do I hold it very stuff o' th' conscience
 To do no contrived murther. I lack iniquity
 Sometimes to do me service. Nine or ten times
5 I had thought t' have yerked him here under the ribs.

 OTHELLO

 'Tis better as it is.

 IAGO   Nay, but he prated,
 And spoke such scurvy and provoking terms
 Against your honor
 That with the little godliness I have
 I did full hard forbear him. But I pray you, sir,
11 Are you fast married? Be assured of this,
12 That the magnifico is much beloved,
13 And hath in his effect a voice potential
14 As double as the Duke's. He will divorce you,
 Or put upon you what restraint and grievance
 The law, with all his might to enforce it on,
 Will give him cable.

 OTHELLO   Let him do his spite.
18 My services which I have done the signiory
19 Shall out-tongue his complaints. 'Tis yet to know –

---

182 *deserve* show gratitude for
I, ii Before the lodgings of Othello 5 *yerked* stabbed 11 *fast* securely
12 *magnifico* grandee (Brabantio) 13 *potential* powerful 14 *double*
doubly influential 18 *signiory* Venetian government 19 *yet to know* still
not generally known

Which, when I know that boasting is an honor,
I shall promulgate – I fetch my life and being
From men of royal siege ; and my demerits   22
May speak unbonneted to as proud a fortune   23
As this that I have reached. For know, Iago,
But that I love the gentle Desdemona,
I would not my unhousèd free condition   26
Put into circumscription and confine
For the sea's worth. But look, what lights come yond ?

IAGO
Those are the raisèd father and his friends.
You were best go in.
OTHELLO   Not I ; I must be found.
My parts, my title, and my perfect soul   31
Shall manifest me rightly. Is it they ?

IAGO
By Janus, I think no.
          Enter Cassio, with torches, Officers.
OTHELLO
The servants of the Duke, and my lieutenant.
The goodness of the night upon you, friends !
What is the news ?
CASSIO   The Duke does greet you, general ;
And he requires your haste-post-haste appearance
Even on the instant.
OTHELLO   What's the matter, think you ?
CASSIO
Something from Cyprus, as I may divine.
It is a business of some heat. The galleys
Have sent a dozen sequent messengers   41
This very night at one another's heels,
And many of the consuls, raised and met,
Are at the Duke's already. You have been hotly called for ;
When, being not at your lodging to be found,

---

22 *siege* rank; *demerits* deserts   23–24 *May speak . . . reached* are equal, I
modestly assert, to those of Desdemona's family   26 *unhousèd* unre-
strained   31 *perfect soul* stainless conscience   41 *sequent* consecutive

The Senate hath sent about three several quests
To search you out.

OTHELLO   'Tis well I am found by you.
I will but spend a word here in the house,
And go with you.   [*Exit.*]

CASSIO   Ancient, what makes he here?

IAGO
50 Faith, he to-night hath boarded a land carack.
If it prove lawful prize, he's made for ever.

CASSIO
I do not understand.

IAGO   He's married.

CASSIO   To who?
        [*Enter Othello.*]

IAGO
Marry, to – Come, captain, will you go?

OTHELLO   Have with you.

CASSIO
Here comes another troop to seek for you.
        *Enter Brabantio, Roderigo, and others with lights
        and weapons.*

IAGO
It is Brabantio. General, be advised.
He comes to bad intent.

OTHELLO   Holla! stand there!

RODERIGO
Signior, it is the Moor.

BRABANTIO   Down with him, thief!
        [*They draw on both sides.*]

IAGO
You, Roderigo! Come, sir, I am for you.

OTHELLO
59 Keep up your bright swords, for the dew will rust them.
Good signior, you shall more command with years
Than with your weapons.

---

50 *carack* treasure ship   59 *Keep up* i.e. sheath

BRABANTIO
O thou foul thief, where hast thou stowed my daughter?
Damned as thou art, thou hast enchanted her!
For I'll refer me to all things of sense,
If she in chains of magic were not bound,
Whether a maid so tender, fair, and happy,
So opposite to marriage that she shunned
The wealthy curlèd darlings of our nation,
Would ever have, t'incur a general mock,
Run from her guardage to the sooty bosom
Of such a thing as thou – to fear, not to delight.
Judge me the world if 'tis not gross in sense   72
That thou hast practiced on her with foul charms,
Abused her delicate youth with drugs or minerals
That weaken motion. I'll have't disputed on;   75
'Tis probable, and palpable to thinking.
I therefore apprehend and do attach thee   77
For an abuser of the world, a practicer
Of arts inhibited and out of warrant.
Lay hold upon him. If he do resist,
Subdue him at his peril.

OTHELLO   Hold your hands,
Both you of my inclining and the rest.
Were it my cue to fight, I should have known it
Without a prompter. Where will you that I go
To answer this your charge?

BRABANTIO   To prison, till fit time
Of law and course of direct session   86
Call thee to answer.

OTHELLO   What if I do obey?
How may the Duke be therewith satisfied,
Whose messengers are here about my side
Upon some present business of the state
To bring me to him?

OFFICER   'Tis true, most worthy signior.

72 *gross in sense* obvious   75 *motion* perception   77 *attach* arrest   86 *direct session* regular trial

The Duke's in council, and your noble self
I am sure is sent for.

BRABANTIO   How? The Duke in council?
In this time of the night? Bring him away.
95   Mine's not an idle cause. The Duke himself,
Or any of my brothers of the state,
Cannot but feel this wrong as 'twere their own;
For if such actions may have passage free,
Bondslaves and pagans shall our statesmen be.   *Exeunt.*

*

I, iii   *Enter Duke and Senators, set at a table, with lights
and Attendants.*

DUKE
1   There is no composition in these news
That gives them credit.

1. SENATOR   Indeed they are disproportionèd.
My letters say a hundred and seven galleys.

DUKE
And mine a hundred forty.

2. SENATOR   And mine two hundred.
5   But though they jump not on a just account –
6   As in these cases where the aim reports
'Tis oft with difference – yet do they all confirm
A Turkish fleet, and bearing up to Cyprus.

DUKE
Nay, it is possible enough to judgment.
10   I do not so secure me in the error
11   But the main article I do approve
In fearful sense.

SAILOR *(within)* What, ho! what, ho! what, ho!

95 *idle* trifling
I, iii The Venetian Senate Chamber   1 *composition* consistency   5 *jump*
agree   6 *aim* conjecture   10 *so secure me* take such comfort   11 *article*
substance; *approve* accept

OFFICER
A messenger from the galleys.
    Enter Sailor.

DUKE   Now, what's the business?

SAILOR
The Turkish preparation makes for Rhodes.
So was I bid report here to the state
By Signior Angelo.

DUKE
How say you by this change?

1. SENATOR   This cannot be
By no assay of reason. 'Tis a pageant   18
To keep us in false gaze. When we consider   19
Th' importancy of Cyprus to the Turk,
And let ourselves again but understand
That, as it more concerns the Turk than Rhodes,
So may he with more facile question bear it,   23
For that it stands not in such warlike brace,   24
But altogether lacks th' abilities
That Rhodes is dressed in – if we make thought of this,
We must not think the Turk is so unskillful
To leave that latest which concerns him first,
Neglecting an attempt of ease and gain
To wake and wage a danger profitless.   30

DUKE
Nay, in all confidence, he's not for Rhodes.

OFFICER
Here is more news.
    Enter a Messenger.

MESSENGER
The Ottomites, reverend and gracious,
Steering with due course toward the isle of Rhodes,
Have there injointed them with an after fleet.

---

18 *assay* test   19 *in false gaze* looking the wrong way   23 *with . . . bear* more easily capture   24 *brace* posture of defense   30 *wake and wage* rouse and risk

I. SENATOR
Ay, so I thought. How many, as you guess?

MESSENGER
37 Of thirty sail; and now they do restem
Their backward course, bearing with frank appearance
Their purposes toward Cyprus. Signior Montano,
Your trusty and most valiant servitor,
With his free duty recommends you thus,
And prays you to believe him.

DUKE
'Tis certain then for Cyprus.
44 Marcus Luccicos, is not he in town?

I. SENATOR
He's now in Florence.

DUKE
Write from us to him; post, post-haste dispatch.

I. SENATOR
Here comes Brabantio and the valiant Moor.
*Enter Brabantio, Othello, Cassio, Iago, Roderigo,
and Officers.*

DUKE
Valiant Othello, we must straight employ you
Against the general enemy Ottoman.
[To Brabantio]
I did not see you. Welcome, gentle signior.
We lacked your counsel and your help to-night.

BRABANTIO
So did I yours. Good your grace, pardon me.
Neither my place, nor aught I heard of business,
Hath raised me from my bed; nor doth the general care
Take hold on me; for my particular grief
56 Is of so floodgate and o'erbearing nature
57 That it engluts and swallows other sorrows,
And it is still itself.

DUKE   Why, what's the matter?

---

37 *restem* steer again **44** *Marcus Luccicos* (presumably a Venetian envoy)
56 *floodgate* torrential **57** *engluts* devours

BRABANTIO
  My daughter! O, my daughter!
ALL   Dead?
BRABANTIO   Ay, to me.
  She is abused, stol'n from me, and corrupted
  By spells and medicines bought of mountebanks;
  For nature so prepost'rously to err,
  Being not deficient, blind, or lame of sense,   63
  Sans witchcraft could not.
DUKE
  Whoe'er he be that in this foul proceeding
  Hath thus beguiled your daughter of herself,
  And you of her, the bloody book of law
  You shall yourself read in the bitter letter
  After your own sense; yea, though our proper son   69
  Stood in your action.   70
BRABANTIO   Humbly I thank your grace.
  Here is the man – this Moor, whom now, it seems,
  Your special mandate for the state affairs
  Hath hither brought.
ALL   We are very sorry for't.
DUKE [to Othello]
  What, in your own part, can you say to this?
BRABANTIO
  Nothing, but this is so.
OTHELLO
  Most potent, grave, and reverend signiors,
  My very noble, and approved good masters,   77
  That I have ta'en away this old man's daughter,
  It is most true; true I have married her.
  The very head and front of my offending
  Hath this extent, no more. Rude am I in my speech,   81
  And little blessed with the soft phrase of peace;
  For since these arms of mine had seven years' pith   83

63 *deficient* feeble-minded   69 *our proper* my own   70 *Stood in your action*
were accused by you   77 *approved* tested by experience   81 *Rude* un-
polished   83 *pith* strength

Till now some nine moons wasted, they have used
Their dearest action in the tented field;
And little of this great world can I speak
More than pertains to feats of broil and battle;
And therefore little shall I grace my cause
In speaking for myself. Yet, by your gracious patience,
90 I will a round unvarnished tale deliver
Of my whole course of love – what drugs, what charms,
What conjuration, and what mighty magic
(For such proceeding am I charged withal)
I won his daughter.

BRABANTIO   A maiden never bold;
95 Of spirit so still and quiet that her motion
Blushed at herself; and she – in spite of nature,
Of years, of country, credit, everything –
To fall in love with what she feared to look on!
It is a judgment maimed and most imperfect
That will confess perfection so could err
Against all rules of nature, and must be driven
102 To find out practices of cunning hell
103 Why this should be. I therefore vouch again
104 That with some mixtures pow'rful o'er the blood,
Or with some dram, conjured to this effect,
He wrought upon her.

DUKE   To vouch this is no proof,
Without more certain and more overt test
108 Than these thin habits and poor likelihoods
109 Of modern seeming do prefer against him.

1.SENATOR
But, Othello, speak.
111 Did you by indirect and forcèd courses
Subdue and poison this young maid's affections?
113 Or came it by request, and such fair question

90 *round* plain 95–96 *her motion Blushed* her own emotions caused her
to blush 102 *practices* plots 103 *vouch* assert 104 *blood* passions
108 *thin habits* slight appearances 109 *modern seeming* everyday supposition 111 *forcèd* violent 113 *question* conversation

As soul to soul affordeth?

OTHELLO   I do beseech you,
Send for the lady to the Sagittary
And let her speak of me before her father.
If you do find me foul in her report,
The trust, the office, I do hold of you
Not only take away, but let your sentence
Even fall upon my life.

DUKE   Fetch Desdemona hither.

OTHELLO
Ancient, conduct them; you best know the place.
                    Exit [Iago, with] two or three [Attendants].
And till she come, as truly as to heaven
I do confess the vices of my blood,
So justly to your grave ears I'll present
How I did thrive in this fair lady's love,
And she in mine.

DUKE
Say it, Othello.

OTHELLO
Her father loved me, oft invited me;
Still questioned me the story of my life   129
From year to year – the battles, sieges, fortunes
That I have passed.
I ran it through, even from my boyish days
To th' very moment that he bade me tell it.
Wherein I spoke of most disastrous chances,
Of moving accidents by flood and field;
Of hairbreadth scapes i' th' imminent deadly breach;
Of being taken by the insolent foe
And sold to slavery; of my redemption thence
And portance in my travels' history;   139
Wherein of anters vast and deserts idle,   140
Rough quarries, rocks, and hills whose heads touch
    heaven,

---

129 *Still* continually   139 *portance* behavior   140 *anters* caves

142 It was my hint to speak – such was the process;
And of the Cannibals that each other eat,
144 The Anthropophagi, and men whose heads
Do grow beneath their shoulders. This to hear
Would Desdemona seriously incline;
But still the house affairs would draw her thence;
Which ever as she could with haste dispatch,
She'ld come again, and with a greedy ear
Devour up my discourse. Which I observing,
151 Took once a pliant hour, and found good means
To draw from her a prayer of earnest heart
153 That I would all my pilgrimage dilate,
154 Whereof by parcels she had something heard,
155 But not intentively. I did consent,
And often did beguile her of her tears
When I did speak of some distressful stroke
That my youth suffered. My story being done,
She gave me for my pains a world of sighs.
She swore, i' faith, 'twas strange, 'twas passing strange;
'Twas pitiful, 'twas wondrous pitiful.
She wished she had not heard it; yet she wished
That heaven had made her such a man. She thanked me;
And bade me, if I had a friend that loved her,
I should but teach him how to tell my story,
166 And that would woo her. Upon this hint I spake.
She loved me for the dangers I had passed,
And I loved her that she did pity them.
This only is the witchcraft I have used.
Here comes the lady. Let her witness it.
          Enter Desdemona, Iago, Attendants.

DUKE
I think this tale would win my daughter too.
Good Brabantio,
Take up this mangled matter at the best.

142 *hint* occasion   144 *Anthropophagi* man-eaters   151 *pliant* propitious
153 *dilate* recount in full   154 *parcels* portions   155 *intentively* with full
attention   166 *hint* opportunity

Men do their broken weapons rather use
Than their bare hands.

BRABANTIO   I pray you hear her speak.
If she confess that she was half the wooer,
Destruction on my head if my bad blame
Light on the man! Come hither, gentle mistress.
Do you perceive in all this noble company
Where most you owe obedience?

DESDEMONA   My noble father,
I do perceive here a divided duty.
To you I am bound for life and education;   182
My life and education both do learn me
How to respect you: you are the lord of duty;
I am hitherto your daughter. But here's my husband;
And so much duty as my mother showed
To you, preferring you before her father,
So much I challenge that I may profess   188
Due to the Moor my lord.

BRABANTIO   God be with you! I have done.
Please it your grace, on to the state affairs.
I had rather to adopt a child than get it.   191
Come hither, Moor.
I here do give thee that with all my heart
Which, but thou hast already, with all my heart
I would keep from thee. For your sake, jewel,   195
I am glad at soul I have no other child;
For thy escape would teach me tyranny,   197
To hang clogs on them. I have done, my lord.

DUKE
Let me speak like yourself and lay a sentence   199
Which, as a grise or step, may help these lovers   200
[Into your favor.]
When remedies are past, the griefs are ended
By seeing the worst, which late on hopes depended.

---

182 *education* upbringing   188 *challenge* claim the right   191 *get* beget
195 *For your sake* because of you   197 *escape* escapade   199 *like yourself*
as you should; *sentence* maxim   200 *grise* step

To mourn a mischief that is past and gone
Is the next way to draw new mischief on.
What cannot be preserved when fortune takes,
Patience her injury a mock'ry makes.
The robbed that smiles steals something from the thief;
He robs himself that spends a bootless grief.

BRABANTIO

210 So let the Turk of Cyprus us beguile:
We lose it not so long as we can smile.
He bears the sentence well that nothing bears
But the free comfort which from thence he hears;
But he bears both the sentence and the sorrow
That to pay grief must of poor patience borrow.
These sentences, to sugar, or to gall,
Being strong on both sides, are equivocal.
But words are words. I never yet did hear
That the bruisèd heart was piercèd through the ear.
Beseech you, now to the affairs of state.

DUKE The Turk with a most mighty preparation makes
222 for Cyprus. Othello, the fortitude of the place is best
known to you; and though we have there a substitute
224 of most allowed sufficiency, yet opinion, a more sover-
eign mistress of effects, throws a more safer voice on you.
226 You must therefore be content to slubber the gloss of
your new fortunes with this more stubborn and
boist'rous expedition.

OTHELLO

The tyrant custom, most grave senators,
Hath made the flinty and steel couch of war
231 My thrice-driven bed of down. I do agnize
A natural and prompt alacrity
I find in hardness; and do undertake
These present wars against the Ottomites.
Most humbly, therefore, bending to your state,

---

222 *fortitude* fortification **224** *allowed* acknowledged; *opinion* public
opinion **226** *slubber* sully **231–33** *agnize . . . hardness* recognize in myself a
natural and easy response to hardship

I crave fit disposition for my wife,
Due reference of place, and exhibition,   237
With such accommodation and besort   238
As levels with her breeding.   239

DUKE   If you please,
Be't at her father's.

BRABANTIO   I will not have it so.

OTHELLO
Nor I.

DESDEMONA   Nor I. I would not there reside,
To put my father in impatient thoughts
By being in his eye. Most gracious Duke,
To my unfolding lend your prosperous ear,   244
And let me find a charter in your voice,
T' assist my simpleness.   246

DUKE
What would you, Desdemona?

DESDEMONA
That I did love the Moor to live with him,
My downright violence, and storm of fortunes,
May trumpet to the world. My heart's subdued
Even to the very quality of my lord.
I saw Othello's visage in his mind,
And to his honors and his valiant parts
Did I my soul and fortunes consecrate.
So that, dear lords, if I be left behind,
A moth of peace, and he go to the war,
The rites for which I love him are bereft me,
And I a heavy interim shall support
By his dear absence. Let me go with him.

OTHELLO
Let her have your voice.
Vouch with me, heaven, I therefore beg it not
To please the palate of my appetite,

---

237 *exhibition* allowance of money   238 *besort* suitable company   239
levels corresponds   244 *prosperous* favorable   246 *simpleness* lack of skill

263 Not to comply with heat – the young affects
   In me defunct – and proper satisfaction;
   But to be free and bounteous to her mind;
   And heaven defend your good souls that you think
   I will your serious and great business scant
   When she is with me. No, when light-winged toys
269 Of feathered Cupid seel with wanton dullness
270 My speculative and officed instruments,
271 That my disports corrupt and taint my business,
   Let housewives make a skillet of my helm,
273 And all indign and base adversities
274 Make head against my estimation!

DUKE
 Be it as you shall privately determine,
 Either for her stay or going. Th' affair cries haste,
 And speed must answer it.

1. SENATOR
 You must away to-night.

OTHELLO   With all my heart.

DUKE
 At nine i' th' morning here we'll meet again.
 Othello, leave some officer behind,
 And he shall our commission bring to you,
 With such things else of quality and respect
283 As doth import you.

OTHELLO   So please your grace, my ancient;
 A man he is of honesty and trust.
 To his conveyance I assign my wife,
 With what else needful your good grace shall think
 To be sent after me.

DUKE   Let it be so.
 Good night to every one.
   [To Brabantio] And, noble signior,

---

263 *heat* passions; *young affects* tendencies of youth 269 *seel*–blind 270 *My . . . instruments* my perceptive and responsible faculties 271 *That* so that 273 *indign* unworthy 274 *estimation* reputation 283 *import* concern

If virtue no delighted beauty lack,   289
Your son-in-law is far more fair than black.

1. SENATOR
Adieu, brave Moor. Use Desdemona well.

BRABANTIO
Look to her, Moor, if thou hast eyes to see :
She has deceived her father, and may thee.
> *Exeunt [Duke, Senators, Officers, &c.].*

OTHELLO
My life upon her faith ! – Honest Iago,
My Desdemona must I leave to thee.
I prithee let thy wife attend on her,
And bring them after in the best advantage.   297
Come, Desdemona. I have but an hour
Of love, of worldly matters and direction,
To spend with thee. We must obey the time.
> *Exit Moor and Desdemona.*

RODERIGO Iago, –
IAGO What say'st thou, noble heart ?
RODERIGO What will I do, think'st thou ?
IAGO Why, go to bed and sleep.
RODERIGO I will incontinently drown myself.   305
IAGO If thou dost, I shall never love thee after. Why, thou
silly gentleman !
RODERIGO It is silliness to live when to live is torment ;
and then have we a prescription to die when death is
our physician.
IAGO O villainous ! I have looked upon the world for four
times seven years ; and since I could distinguish betwixt a benefit and an injury, I never found man that
knew how to love himself. Ere I would say I would
drown myself for the love of a guinea hen, I would
change my humanity with a baboon.
RODERIGO What should I do ? I confess it is my shame
to be so fond, but it is not in my virtue to amend it.

---

289 *delighted* delightful   297 *in the best advantage* at the best opportunity
305 *incontinently* forthwith

IAGO Virtue? a fig! 'Tis in ourselves that we are thus or
thus. Our bodies are our gardens, to the which our wills
are gardeners; so that if we will plant nettles or sow
lettuce, set hyssop and weed up thyme, supply it with
323   one gender of herbs or distract it with many – either to
have it sterile with idleness or manured with industry –
325   why, the power and corrigible authority of this lies in
our wills. If the balance of our lives had not one scale
327   of reason to poise another of sensuality, the blood and
baseness of our natures would conduct us to most
preposterous conclusions. But we have reason to cool our
330   raging motions, our carnal stings, our unbitted lusts;
331   whereof I take this that you call love to be a sect or scion.
RODERIGO It cannot be.
IAGO It is merely a lust of the blood and a permission of
the will. Come, be a man! Drown thyself? Drown cats
and blind puppies! I have professed me thy friend, and I
confess me knit to thy deserving with cables of perdurable
toughness. I could never better stead thee than now. Put
338   money in thy purse. Follow thou the wars; defeat thy
favor with an usurped beard. I say, put money in thy
purse. It cannot be that Desdemona should long continue her love to the Moor – put money in thy purse – nor
he his to her. It was a violent commencement in her, and
343   thou shalt see an answerable sequestration – put but
money in thy purse. These Moors are changeable in their
wills – fill thy purse with money. The food that to him
now is as luscious as locusts shall be to him shortly as bit-
347   ter as coloquintida. She must change for youth: when she
is sated with his body, she will find the error of her choice.
[She must have change, she must.] Therefore put money
in thy purse. If thou wilt needs damn thyself, do it a more

323 *gender* species   325 *corrigible authority* corrective power   327 *poise*
counterbalance   327–28 *blood and baseness* animal instincts   330 *motions*
appetites; *unbitted* uncontrolled   331 *sect or scion* offshoot, cutting   338–39
defeat thy favor spoil thy appearance   343 *sequestration* estrangement   347
coloquintida a medicine

delicate way than drowning. Make all the money thou 351
canst. If sanctimony and a frail vow betwixt an erring 352
barbarian and a supersubtle Venetian be not too hard for
my wits and all the tribe of hell, thou shalt enjoy her.
Therefore make money. A pox of drowning thyself! 'Tis
clean out of the way. Seek thou rather to be hanged in
compassing thy joy than to be drowned and go without
her.

RODERIGO Wilt thou be fast to my hopes, if I depend on
the issue?

IAGO Thou art sure of me. Go, make money. I have told
thee often, and I retell thee again and again, I hate the
Moor. My cause is hearted; thine hath no less reason. 362
Let us be conjunctive in our revenge against him. If
thou canst cuckold him, thou dost thyself a pleasure, me
a sport. There are many events in the womb of time,
which will be delivered. Traverse, go, provide thy 366
money! We will have more of this to-morrow. Adieu.

RODERIGO Where shall we meet i' th' morning?

IAGO At my lodging.

RODERIGO I'll be with thee betimes.

IAGO Go to, farewell. – Do you hear, Roderigo?

[RODERIGO What say you?

IAGO No more of drowning, do you hear?

RODERIGO I am changed.

IAGO Go to, farewell. Put money enough in your purse.]

RODERIGO I'll sell all my land.   *Exit.*

IAGO

    Thus do I ever make my fool my purse;
    For I mine own gained knowledge should profane
    If I would time expend with such a snipe   379
    But for my sport and profit. I hate the Moor;
    And it is thought abroad that 'twixt my sheets
    H'as done my office. I know not if 't be true;
    But I, for mere suspicion in that kind,

351 *Make* raise   352 *erring* wandering   362 *My cause is hearted* my heart
is in it   366 *Traverse* forward march   379 *snipe* fool

384 Will do as if for surety. He holds me well;
The better shall my purpose work on him.
Cassio's a proper man. Let me see now:

387 To get his place, and to plume up my will
In double knavery – How, how? – Let's see: –
After some time, to abuse Othello's ears
That he is too familiar with his wife.

391 He hath a person and a smooth dispose
To be suspected – framed to make women false.

393 The Moor is of a free and open nature
That thinks men honest that but seem to be so;
And will as tenderly be led by th' nose
As asses are.
I have't! It is engend'red! Hell and night
Must bring this monstrous birth to the world's light.

                                                           Exit.

                              *

II, i   *Enter Montano and two Gentlemen.*

MONTANO
        What from the cape can you discern at sea?

1. GENTLEMAN
        Nothing at all: it is a high-wrought flood.
        I cannot 'twixt the heaven and the main
        Descry a sail.

MONTANO
        Methinks the wind hath spoke aloud at land;
        A fuller blast ne'er shook our battlements.
        If it hath ruffianed so upon the sea,
        What ribs of oak, when mountains melt on them,
    9   Can hold the mortise? What shall we hear of this?

    2. GENTLEMAN
   10   A segregation of the Turkish fleet.

---

384 *well* in high regard   387 *plume up* gratify   391 *dispose* manner   393
free frank
II, i An open place in Cyprus, near the harbor   9 *hold the mortise* hold
their joints together   10 *segregation* scattering

For do but stand upon the foaming shore,
The chidden billow seems to pelt the clouds;
The wind-shaked surge, with high and monstrous mane,
Seems to cast water on the burning Bear
And quench the Guards of th' ever-fixèd pole.   15
I never did like molestation view   16
On the enchafèd flood.

MONTANO   If that the Turkish fleet
Be not ensheltered and embayed, they are drowned;
It is impossible to bear it out.
        Enter a third Gentleman.

3. GENTLEMAN
News, lads! Our wars are done.
The desperate tempest hath so banged the Turks
That their designment halts. A noble ship of Venice   22
Hath seen a grievous wrack and sufferance   23
On most part of their fleet.

MONTANO
How? Is this true?

3. GENTLEMAN   The ship is here put in,
A Veronesa; Michael Cassio,   26
Lieutenant to the warlike Moor Othello,
Is come on shore; the Moor himself at sea,
And is in full commission here for Cyprus.

MONTANO
I am glad on't. 'Tis a worthy governor.

3. GENTLEMAN
But this same Cassio, though he speak of comfort
Touching the Turkish loss, yet he looks sadly
And prays the Moor be safe, for they were parted
With foul and violent tempest.

MONTANO   Pray heaven he be;
For I have served him, and the man commands
Like a full soldier. Let's to the seaside, ho!

---

15 *Guards* stars near the North Star; *pole* polestar   16 *molestation* tumult
22 *designment halts* plan is crippled   23 *sufferance* disaster   26 *Veronesa*
ship furnished by Verona

As well to see the vessel that's come in
As to throw out our eyes for brave Othello,
Even till we make the main and th' aerial blue
40   An indistinct regard.

3 . GENTLEMAN   Come, let's do so ;
For every minute is expectancy
Of more arrivance.
        Enter Cassio.

CASSIO
Thanks, you the valiant of this warlike isle,
That so approve the Moor ! O, let the heavens
Give him defense against the elements,
For I have lost him on a dangerous sea !

MONTANO
Is he well shipped ?

CASSIO
His bark is stoutly timbered, and his pilot
Of very expert and approved allowance ;
50   Therefore my hopes, not surfeited to death,
51   Stand in bold cure.
        (Within) A sail, a sail, a sail !
        Enter a Messenger.

CASSIO
What noise ?

MESSENGER
The town is empty ; on the brow o' th' sea
Stand ranks of people, and they cry 'A sail !'

CASSIO
My hopes do shape him for the governor.
        A shot.

2 . GENTLEMAN
They do discharge their shot of courtesy :
Our friends at least.

CASSIO   I pray you, sir, go forth
And give us truth who 'tis that is arrived.

40 *An indistinct regard* indistinguishable 50 *surfeited to death* over-
indulged 51 *in bold cure* a good chance of fulfillment

2. GENTLEMAN
  I shall.   *Exit.*

MONTANO
  But, good lieutenant, is your general wived?

CASSIO
  Most fortunately. He hath achieved a maid
  That paragons description and wild fame;   62
  One that excels the quirks of blazoning pens,   63
  And in th' essential vesture of creation   64
  Does tire the ingener.
      Enter Second Gentleman.
                     How now? Who has put in?

2. GENTLEMAN
  'Tis one Iago, ancient to the general.

CASSIO
  H'as had most favorable and happy speed:
  Tempests themselves, high seas, and howling winds,
  The guttered rocks and congregated sands,   69
  Traitors ensteeped to clog the guiltless keel,   70
  As having sense of beauty, do omit
  Their mortal natures, letting go safely by   72
  The divine Desdemona.

MONTANO   What is she?

CASSIO
  She that I spake of, our great captain's captain,
  Left in the conduct of the bold Iago,
  Whose footing here anticipates our thoughts   76
  A se'nnight's speed. Great Jove, Othello guard,   77
  And swell his sail with thine own pow'rful breath,
  That he may bless this bay with his tall ship,
  Make love's quick pants in Desdemona's arms,
  Give renewed fire to our extincted spirits,
  [And bring all Cyprus comfort!]

---

62 *paragons* surpasses **63** *quirks* ingenuities; *blazoning* describing **64–65**
And . . . ingener merely to describe her as God made her exhausts her praiser
69 *guttered* jagged **70** *ensteeped* submerged **72** *mortal* deadly **76**
footing landing **77** *se'nnight's* week's

Enter Desdemona, Iago, Roderigo, and Emilia [with
   Attendants].   O, behold!
   The riches of the ship is come on shore!
84 You men of Cyprus, let her have your knees.
   Hail to thee, lady! and the grace of heaven,
   Before, behind thee, and on every hand,
   Enwheel thee round!
DESDEMONA   I thank you, valiant Cassio.
   What tidings can you tell me of my lord?
CASSIO
   He is not yet arrived; nor know I aught
   But that he's well and will be shortly here.
DESDEMONA
   O but I fear! How lost you company?
CASSIO
   The great contention of the sea and skies
   Parted our fellowship.
        (Within) A sail, a sail! *[A shot.]*
                         But hark. A sail!
2. GENTLEMAN
   They give their greeting to the citadel;
   This likewise is a friend.
CASSIO   See for the news.
                         [Exit Gentleman.]
   Good ancient, you are welcome.
        [To Emilia]   Welcome, mistress. –
   Let it not gall your patience, good Iago,
   That I extend my manners. 'Tis my breeding
99 That gives me this bold show of courtesy.
        [Kisses Emilia.]
IAGO
   Sir, would she give you so much of her lips
   As of her tongue she oft bestows on me,
   You would have enough.
DESDEMONA   Alas, she has no speech!

---

84 *knees* i.e. kneeling   **99** s.d. *Kisses Emilia* (kissing was a common Elizabethan form of social courtesy)

IAGO

In faith, too much.
I find it still when I have list to sleep.
Marry, before your ladyship, I grant,
She puts her tongue a little in her heart
And chides with thinking.

EMILIA

You have little cause to say so.

IAGO

Come on, come on! You are pictures out of doors,
Bells in your parlors, wildcats in your kitchens,
Saints in your injuries, devils being offended,
Players in your housewifery, and housewives in your   112
    beds.

DESDEMONA

O, fie upon thee, slanderer!

IAGO

Nay, it is true, or else I am a Turk:
You rise to play, and go to bed to work.

EMILIA

You shall not write my praise.

IAGO   No, let me not.

DESDEMONA

What wouldst thou write of me, if thou shouldst praise
    me?

IAGO

O gentle lady, do not put me to't,
For I am nothing if not critical.

DESDEMONA

Come on, assay. – There's one gone to the harbor?   120

IAGO

Ay, madam.

DESDEMONA

I am not merry; but I do beguile
The thing I am by seeming otherwise. –

112 *housewifery* housekeeping; *housewives* hussies   120 *assay* try

57

Come, how wouldst thou praise me ?

IAGO

I am about it ; but indeed my invention

126   Comes from my pate as birdlime does from frieze –
It plucks out brains and all. But my Muse labors,
And thus she is delivered :
If she be fair and wise, fairness and wit –
The one 's for use, the other useth it.

DESDEMONA

131   Well praised ! How if she be black and witty ?

IAGO

If she be black, and thereto have a wit,
She'll find a white that shall her blackness fit.

DESDEMONA

Worse and worse !

EMILIA

How if fair and foolish ?

IAGO

She never yet was foolish that was fair,

137   For even her folly helped her to an heir.

138 DESDEMONA   These are old fond paradoxes to make fools
laugh i' th' alehouse. What miserable praise hast thou

140   for her that's foul and foolish ?

IAGO

There's none so foul, and foolish thereunto,
But does foul pranks which fair and wise ones do.

DESDEMONA   O heavy ignorance ! Thou praisest the
worst best. But what praise couldst thou bestow on a
deserving woman indeed – one that in the authority of

146   her merit did justly put on the vouch of very malice
itself ?

IAGO

She that was ever fair, and never proud ;
Had tongue at will, and yet was never loud ;

126 *birdlime* a sticky paste; *frieze* rough cloth   131 *black* brunette   137
folly wantonness   138 *fond* foolish   140 *foul* ugly   146 *put on the vouch*
compel the approval

Never lacked gold, and yet went never gay;
Fled from her wish, and yet said 'Now I may';
She that, being ang'red, her revenge being nigh,
Bade her wrong stay, and her displeasure fly;
She that in wisdom never was so frail
To change the cod's head for the salmon's tail;   154
She that could think, and ne'er disclose her mind;
See suitors following, and not look behind:
She was a wight (if ever such wight were)—

DESDEMONA To do what?

IAGO
To suckle fools and chronicle small beer.   159

DESDEMONA O most lame and impotent conclusion! Do
not learn of him, Emilia, though he be thy husband.
How say you, Cassio? Is he not a most profane and   162
liberal counsellor?

CASSIO He speaks home, madam. You may relish him   164
more in the soldier than in the scholar.

IAGO [aside] He takes her by the palm. Ay, well said,
whisper! With as little a web as this will I ensnare as
great a fly as Cassio. Ay, smile upon her, do! I will gyve   168
thee in thine own courtship. – You say true; 'tis so, indeed! – If such tricks as these strip you out of your lieu-
tenantry, it had been better you had not kissed your
three fingers so oft – which now again you are most apt
to play the sir in. Very good! well kissed! an excellent   173
courtesy! 'Tis so, indeed. Yet again your fingers to your
lips? Would they were clyster pipes for your sake!   175
(Trumpet within.) The Moor! I know his trumpet.

CASSIO 'Tis truly so.

DESDEMONA Let's meet him and receive him.

CASSIO Lo, where he comes.

154 To . . . tail i.e. to exchange the good for the poor but expensive   159
chronicle small beer keep petty household accounts   162–63 profane and
liberal worldly and licentious   164 home bluntly   168–69 gyve . . . courtship
manacle you by means of your courtly manners   173 sir courtly gentleman
175 clyster pipes syringes

Enter Othello and Attendants.

OTHELLO
O my fair warrior!

DESDEMONA   My dear Othello!

OTHELLO
It gives me wonder great as my content
To see you here before me. O my soul's joy!
If after every tempest come such calms,
May the winds blow till they have wakened death!
And let the laboring bark climb hills of seas
Olympus-high, and duck again as low
As hell's from heaven! If it were now to die,
188   'Twere now to be most happy; for I fear
My soul hath her content so absolute
That not another comfort like to this
Succeeds in unknown fate.

DESDEMONA   The heavens forbid
But that our loves and comforts should increase
Even as our days do grow.

OTHELLO   Amen to that, sweet powers!
I cannot speak enough of this content;
It stops me here; it is too much of joy.
And this, and this, the greatest discords be
        They kiss.
That e'er our hearts shall make!

IAGO [*aside*]   O, you are well tuned now!
198   But I'll set down the pegs that make this music,
As honest as I am.

OTHELLO   Come, let us to the castle.
News, friends! Our wars are done; the Turks are
        drowned.
How does my old acquaintance of this isle? –
202   Honey, you shall be well desired in Cyprus;
I have found great love amongst them. O my sweet,
I prattle out of fashion, and I dote

188 *happy* fortunate   198 *set down* loosen   202 *well desired* warmly
welcomed

In mine own comforts. I prithee, good Iago,
Go to the bay and disembark my coffers.
Bring thou the master to the citadel;   207
He is a good one, and his worthiness
Does challenge much respect. – Come, Desdemona,   209
Once more well met at Cyprus.

       Exit Othello [with all but Iago and Roderigo].

IAGO *[to an Attendant, who goes out]* Do thou meet me
presently at the harbor. *[to Roderigo]* Come hither. If
thou be'st valiant (as they say base men being in love
have then a nobility in their natures more than is native
to them), list me. The lieutenant to-night watches on
the court of guard. First, I must tell thee this: Des-   216
demona is directly in love with him.

RODERIGO With him? Why, 'tis not possible.

IAGO Lay thy finger thus, and let thy soul be instructed.   219
Mark me with what violence she first loved the Moor,
but for bragging and telling her fantastical lies; and will
she love him still for prating? Let not thy discreet heart
think it. Her eye must be fed; and what delight shall she
have to look on the devil? When the blood is made dull
with the act of sport, there should be, again to inflame it
and to give satiety a fresh appetite, loveliness in favor,
sympathy in years, manners, and beauties; all which the
Moor is defective in. Now for want of these required
conveniences, her delicate tenderness will find itself   229
abused, begin to heave the gorge, disrelish and abhor the   230
Moor. Very nature will instruct her in it and compel her
to some second choice. Now sir, this granted – as it is a
most pregnant and unforced position – who stands so   233
eminent in the degree of this fortune as Cassio does? A
knave very voluble; no further conscionable than in put-   235
ting on the mere form of civil and humane seeming for   236

---

207 *master* ship captain 209 *challenge* deserve 216 *court of guard* head-
quarters 219 *thus* i.e. on your lips 229 *conveniences* compatibilities
230 *heave the gorge* be nauseated 233 *pregnant* evident 235 *conscionable*
conscientious 236 *humane* polite

237 the better compassing of his salt and most hidden loose
238 affection? Why, none! why, none! A slipper and subtle
knave; a finder-out of occasions; that has an eye can
stamp and counterfeit advantages, though true advantage never present itself; a devilish knave! Besides, the
knave is handsome, young, and hath all those requisites
in him that folly and green minds look after. A pestilent
complete knave! and the woman hath found him already.

RODERIGO I cannot believe that in her; she's full of most
246 blessed condition.

IAGO Blessed fig's-end! The wine she drinks is made of
grapes. If she had been blessed, she would never have
loved the Moor. Blessed pudding! Didst thou not see
her paddle with the palm of his hand? Didst not mark
that?

RODERIGO Yes, that I did; but that was but courtesy.

IAGO Lechery, by this hand! an index and obscure prologue to the history of lust and foul thoughts. They met
so near with their lips that their breaths embraced to-
255 gether. Villainous thoughts, Roderigo! When these mutualities so marshal the way, hard at hand comes the
257 master and main exercise, th' incorporate conclusion.
Pish! But, sir, be you ruled by me: I have brought you
from Venice. Watch you to-night; for the command,
I'll lay 't upon you. Cassio knows you not. I'll not be far
from you: do you find some occasion to anger Cassio,
262 either by speaking too loud, or tainting his discipline, or
from what other course you please which the time shall
more favorably minister.

RODERIGO Well.

266 IAGO Sir, he's rash and very sudden in choler, and haply
with his truncheon may strike at you. Provoke him that
he may; for even out of that will I cause these of Cyprus

---

237 *salt* lecherous 238 *slipper* slippery 246 *condition* character 255
mutualities exchanges 257 *incorporate* carnal 262 *tainting* discrediting
266 *sudden in choler* violent in anger

to mutiny; whose qualification shall come into no true 269
taste again but by the displanting of Cassio. So shall you
have a shorter journey to your desires by the means I
shall then have to prefer them; and the impediment 272
most profitably removed without the which there were
no expectation of our prosperity.

RODERIGO I will do this if you can bring it to any opportunity.

IAGO I warrant thee. Meet me by and by at the citadel; I
must fetch his necessaries ashore. Farewell.

RODERIGO Adieu.   *Exit.*

IAGO

    That Cassio loves her, I do well believe't;
    That she loves him, 'tis apt and of great credit.   281
    The Moor, howbeit that I endure him not,
    Is of a constant, loving, noble nature,
    And I dare think he'll prove to Desdemona
    A most dear husband. Now I do love her too;
    Not out of absolute lust, though peradventure
    I stand accountant for as great a sin,   287
    But partly led to diet my revenge,   288
    For that I do suspect the lusty Moor
    Hath leaped into my seat; the thought whereof
    Doth, like a poisonous mineral, gnaw my inwards;
    And nothing can or shall content my soul
    Till I am evened with him, wife for wife;
    Or failing so, yet that I put the Moor
    At least into a jealousy so strong
    That judgment cannot cure. Which thing to do,
    If this poor trash of Venice, whom I trash   297
    For his quick hunting, stand the putting on,   298
    I'll have our Michael Cassio on the hip,   299

269 *qualification* appeasement   269–70 *true taste* satisfactory state   272
prefer advance   281 *apt* probable   287 *accountant* accountable   288 *diet*
feed   297 *I trash* I weight down (in order to keep under control)   298
For in order to develop; *stand the putting on* responds to my inciting   299
on the hip at my mercy

300 Abuse him to the Moor in the rank garb
    (For I fear Cassio with my nightcap too),
    Make the Moor thank me, love me, and reward me
    For making him egregiously an ass
304 And practicing upon his peace and quiet
    Even to madness. 'Tis here, but yet confused:
    Knavery's plain face is never seen till used.   *Exit.*

*

II, ii   *Enter Othello's Herald, with a proclamation.*
    HERALD It is Othello's pleasure, our noble and valiant
    general, that, upon certain tidings now arrived, import-
  3 ing the mere perdition of the Turkish fleet, every man
    put himself into triumph; some to dance, some to make
    bonfires, each man to what sport and revels his addic-
    tion leads him. For, besides these beneficial news, it is
    the celebration of his nuptial. So much was his pleasure
  8 should be proclaimed. All offices are open, and there is
    full liberty of feasting from the present hour of five till
    the bell have told eleven. Heaven bless the isle of
    Cyprus and our noble general Othello!   *Exit.*

*

II, iii   *Enter Othello, Desdemona, Cassio, and Attendants.*
    OTHELLO
        Good Michael, look you to the guard to-night.
        Let's teach ourselves that honorable stop,
        Not to outsport discretion.
    CASSIO
        Iago hath direction what to do;
        But not withstanding, with my personal eye

300 *rank garb* gross manner   304 *practicing upon* plotting against
II, ii A street in Cyprus   3 *mere perdition* complete destruction   8 *offices*
kitchens and storerooms
II, iii The Cyprian castle

Will I look to't.

OTHELLO   Iago is most honest.
Michael, good night. To-morrow with your earliest
Let me have speech with you.
          [*To Desdemona*]   Come, my dear love.
The purchase made, the fruits are to ensue;
That profit's yet to come 'tween me and you. –
Good night.
          Exit [Othello with Desdemona and Attendants].
          Enter Iago.

CASSIO Welcome, Iago. We must to the watch.

IAGO Not this hour, lieutenant; 'tis not yet ten o' th'
clock. Our general cast us thus early for the love of his   14
Desdemona; who let us not therefore blame. He hath
not yet made wanton the night with her, and she is
sport for Jove.

CASSIO She's a most exquisite lady.

IAGO And, I'll warrant her, full of game.

CASSIO Indeed, she's a most fresh and delicate creature.

IAGO What an eye she has! Methinks it sounds a parley to
provocation.

CASSIO An inviting eye; and yet methinks right modest.

IAGO And when she speaks, is it not an alarum to love?

CASSIO She is indeed perfection.

IAGO Well, happiness to their sheets! Come, lieutenant, I
have a stoup of wine, and here without are a brace of   27
Cyprus gallants that would fain have a measure to the
health of black Othello.

CASSIO Not to-night, good Iago. I have very poor and unhappy brains for drinking; I could well wish courtesy
would invent some other custom of entertainment.

IAGO O, they are our friends. But one cup! I'll drink for
you.

CASSIO I have drunk but one cup to-night, and that was
craftily qualified too; and behold what innovation it   36

14 *cast* dismissed   27 *stoup* two-quart tankard   36 *qualified* diluted;
innovation disturbance

65

makes here. I am unfortunate in the infirmity and dare
not task my weakness with any more.

IAGO What, man! 'Tis a night of revels: the gallants
desire it.

CASSIO Where are they?

IAGO Here at the door; I pray you call them in.

CASSIO I'll do't, but it dislikes me.   *Exit.*

IAGO
If I can fasten but one cup upon him
With that which he hath drunk to-night already,
He'll be as full of quarrel and offense
As my young mistress' dog. Now my sick fool Roderigo,
Whom love hath turned almost the wrong side out,
To Desdemona hath to-night caroused
50   Potations pottle-deep; and he's to watch.
Three lads of Cyprus – noble swelling spirits,
52   That hold their honors in a wary distance,
53   The very elements of this warlike isle –
Have I to-night flustered with flowing cups,
And they watch too. Now, 'mongst this flock of
     drunkards
Am I to put our Cassio in some action
That may offend the isle.
       *Enter Cassio, Montano, and Gentlemen [; Servants
       following with wine].*
                           But here they come.
If consequence do but approve my dream,
My boat sails freely, both with wind and stream.

60 CASSIO 'Fore God, they have given me a rouse already.

MONTANO Good faith, a little one; not past a pint, as I
am a soldier.

IAGO Some wine, ho!
     [Sings]   And let me the canakin clink, clink;
               And let me the canakin clink.

---

50 *pottle-deep* bottoms up   **52** *That . . . distance* very sensitive about their
honor   **53** *very elements* true representatives   **60** *rouse* bumper

      A soldier's a man;
      A life's but a span,
     Why then, let a soldier drink.
Some wine, boys!   70

CASSIO 'Fore God, an excellent song!

IAGO I learned it in England, where indeed they are most potent in potting. Your Dane, your German, and your swag-bellied Hollander – Drink, ho! – are nothing to your English.

CASSIO Is your Englishman so expert in his drinking?

IAGO Why, he drinks you with facility your Dane dead drunk; he sweats not to overthrow your Almain; he gives your Hollander a vomit ere the next pottle can be filled.

CASSIO To the health of our general!

MONTANO I am for it, lieutenant, and I'll do you justice.

IAGO O sweet England!

  [Sings]   King Stephen was a worthy peer;
          His breeches cost him but a crown;
          He held 'em sixpence all too dear,
            With that he called the tailor lown.   87
          He was a wight of high renown,
            And thou art but of low degree.
        'Tis pride that pulls the country down;
           Then take thine auld cloak about thee.
Some wine, ho!

CASSIO 'Fore God, this is a more exquisite song than the other.

IAGO Will you hear't again?

CASSIO No, for I hold him to be unworthy of his place that does those things. Well, God's above all; and there 97 be souls must be saved, and there be souls must not be saved.

IAGO It's true, good lieutenant.

---

87 *lown* rascal   97 *does . . . things* i.e. behaves in this fashion

CASSIO For mine own part – no offense to the general,
nor any man of quality – I hope to be saved.

IAGO And so do I too, lieutenant.

CASSIO Ay, but, by your leave, not before me. The lieutenant is to be saved before the ancient. Let's have no
more of this; let's to our affairs. – God forgive us our
sins! – Gentlemen, let's look to our business. Do not
think, gentlemen, I am drunk. This is my ancient; this
is my right hand, and this is my left. I am not drunk now.
110 I can stand well enough, and I speak well enough.

ALL Excellent well!

CASSIO Why, very well then. You must not think then
that I am drunk.   *Exit*.

MONTANO
To th' platform, masters. Come, let's set the watch.

IAGO
You see this fellow that is gone before.
He's a soldier fit to stand by Caesar
And give direction; and do but see his vice.
118   'Tis to his virtue a just equinox,
The one as long as th' other. 'Tis pity of him.
I fear the trust Othello puts him in,
On some odd time of his infirmity,
Will shake this island.

MONTANO   But is he often thus?

IAGO
'Tis evermore his prologue to his sleep:
124   He'll watch the horologe a double set
If drink rock not his cradle.

MONTANO   It were well
The general were put in mind of it.
Perhaps he sees it not, or his good nature
Prizes the virtue that appears in Cassio
And looks not on his evils. Is not this true?
          Enter Roderigo.

118 *just equinox* exact equivalent   124 *watch . . . set* stay awake twice
around the clock

IAGO *[aside to him]*
How now, Roderigo?
I pray you after the lieutenant, go! *Exit Roderigo.*
MONTANO
And 'tis great pity that the noble Moor
Should hazard such a place as his own second
With one of an ingraft infirmity.   134
It were an honest action to say
So to the Moor.
IAGO   Not I, for this fair island!
I do love Cassio well and would do much
To cure him of this evil.
            (Within) Help! help!
                              But hark! What noise?
      Enter Cassio, driving in Roderigo.
CASSIO
Zounds, you rogue! you rascal!
MONTANO
What's the matter, lieutenant?
CASSIO   A knave teach me my duty?
I'll beat the knave into a twiggen bottle.   141
RODERIGO
Beat me?
CASSIO   Dost thou prate, rogue?
      [Strikes him.]
MONTANO   Nay, good lieutenant!
      [Stays him.]
I pray you, sir, hold your hand.
CASSIO   Let me go, sir,
Or I'll knock you o'er the mazzard.   144
MONTANO   Come, come, you're drunk!
CASSIO Drunk?
      They fight.
IAGO *[aside to Roderigo]*
Away, I say! Go out and cry a mutiny! *Exit Roderigo.*

134 *ingraft* i.e. ingrained   141 *twiggen* wicker-covered   144 *mazzard* head

Nay, good lieutenant. God's will, gentlemen!
Help, ho! – lieutenant – sir – Montano – sir –
Help, masters! – Here's a goodly watch indeed!
    A bell rung.
Who's that which rings the bell? Diablo, ho!
151 The town will rise. God's will, lieutenant, hold!
You'll be shamed for ever.
    Enter Othello and Gentlemen with weapons.

OTHELLO   What is the matter here?

MONTANO
Zounds, I bleed still. I am hurt to th' death.
He dies!

OTHELLO
Hold for your lives!

IAGO
Hold, hold! Lieutenant – sir – Montano – gentlemen!
Have you forgot all sense of place and duty?
Hold! The general speaks to you. Hold, for shame!

OTHELLO
Why, how now, ho? From whence ariseth this?
Are we turned Turks, and to ourselves do that
Which heaven hath forbid the Ottomites?
For Christian shame put by this barbarous brawl!
163 He that stirs next to carve for his own rage
Holds his soul light; he dies upon his motion.
Silence that dreadful bell! It frights the isle
166 From her propriety. What is the matter, masters?
Honest Iago, that looks dead with grieving,
Speak: Who began this? On thy love, I charge thee.

IAGO
I do not know. Friends all, but now, even now,
170 In quarter, and in terms like bride and groom
Devesting them for bed; and then, but now –
As if some planet had unwitted men –
Swords out, and tilting one at other's breast

151 *rise* grow riotous 163 *carve for* indulge 166 *propriety* proper self
170 *quarter* friendliness

In opposition bloody. I cannot speak
Any beginning to this peevish odds, 175
And would in action glorious I had lost
Those legs that brought me to a part of it!

OTHELLO
How comes it, Michael, you are thus forgot?

CASSIO
I pray you pardon me; I cannot speak.

OTHELLO
Worthy Montano, you were wont to be civil;
The gravity and stillness of your youth
The world hath noted, and your name is great
In mouths of wisest censure. What's the matter 183
That you unlace your reputation thus 184
And spend your rich opinion for the name 185
Of a night-brawler? Give me answer to it.

MONTANO
Worthy Othello, I am hurt to danger.
Your officer, Iago, can inform you,
While I spare speech, which something now offends me, 189
Of all that I do know; nor know I aught
By me that's said or done amiss this night,
Unless self-charity be sometimes a vice,
And to defend ourselves it be a sin
When violence assails us.

OTHELLO   Now, by heaven,
My blood begins my safer guides to rule, 195
And passion, having my best judgment collied, 196
Assays to lead the way. If I once stir 197
Or do but lift this arm, the best of you
Shall sink in my rebuke. Give me to know
How this foul rout began, who set it on;
And he that is approved in this offense, 201
Though he had twinned with me, both at a birth,

175 *peevish odds* childish quarrel   183 *censure* judgment   184 *unlace* undo
185 *rich opinion* high reputation   189 *offends* pains   195 *blood* passion   196
collied darkened   197 *Assays* tries   201 *approved in* proved guilty of

Shall lose me. What! in a town of war,
Yet wild, the people's hearts brimful of fear,
205 To manage private and domestic quarrel?
In night, and on the court and guard of safety?
'Tis monstrous. Iago, who began't?

MONTANO

208 If partially affined, or leagued in office,
Thou dost deliver more or less than truth,
Thou art no soldier.

IAGO   Touch me not so near.
I had rather have this tongue cut from my mouth
Than it should do offense to Michael Cassio;
Yet I persuade myself, to speak the truth
Shall nothing wrong him. This it is, general.
Montano and myself being in speech,
There comes a fellow crying out for help,
And Cassio following him with determined sword
218 To execute upon him. Sir, this gentleman
Steps in to Cassio and entreats his pause.
Myself the crying fellow did pursue,
Lest by his clamor – as it so fell out –
The town might fall in fright. He, swift of foot,
Outran my purpose; and I returned then rather
For that I heard the clink and fall of swords,
225 And Cassio high in oath; which till to-night
I ne'er might say before. When I came back –
For this was brief – I found them close together
At blow and thrust, even as again they were
When you yourself did part them.
More of this matter cannot I report;
But men are men; the best sometimes forget.
Though Cassio did some little wrong to him,
As men in rage strike those that wish them best,
Yet surely Cassio I believe received
From him that fled some strange indignity,

205 *manage* carry on   **208** *partially . . . office* prejudiced by comradeship or official relations   **218** *execute* work his will   **225** *high in oath* cursing

Which patience could not pass.   236

OTHELLO   I know, Iago,
Thy honesty and love doth mince this matter,
Making it light to Cassio. Cassio, I love thee;
But never more be officer of mine.
        Enter Desdemona, attended.
Look if my gentle love be not raised up!
I'll make thee an example.

DESDEMONA   What's the matter?

OTHELLO
All's well now, sweeting; come away to bed.
        [To Montano]
Sir, for your hurts, myself will be your surgeon.
Lead him off.
        [Montano is led off.]
Iago, look with care about the town
And silence those whom this vile brawl distracted.   246
Come, Desdemona; 'tis the soldiers' life
To have their balmy slumbers waked with strife.
                    Exit [with all but Iago and Cassio].

IAGO What, are you hurt, lieutenant?

CASSIO Ay, past all surgery.

IAGO Marry, God forbid!

CASSIO Reputation, reputation, reputation! O, I have
lost my reputation! I have lost the immortal part of
myself, and what remains is bestial. My reputation,
Iago, my reputation!

IAGO As I am an honest man, I thought you had received
some bodily wound. There is more sense in that than in
reputation. Reputation is an idle and most false imposi-
tion; oft got without merit and lost without deserving.
You have lost no reputation at all unless you repute yourself such a loser. What, man! there are ways to recover 261
the general again. You are but now cast in his mood – a 262
punishment more in policy than in malice, even so as

236 *pass* pass over, ignore   246 *distracted* excited   261 *recover* regain favor
with   262 *cast in his mood* dismissed because of his anger

73

one would beat his offenseless dog to affright an imperious lion. Sue to him again, and he's yours.

CASSIO I will rather sue to be despised than to deceive so
good a commander with so slight, so drunken, and so
268 indiscreet an officer. Drunk! and speak parrot! and
269 squabble! swagger! swear! and discourse fustian with
one's own shadow! O thou invisible spirit of wine, if
thou hast no name to be known by, let us call thee devil!

IAGO What was he that you followed with your sword?
What had he done to you?

CASSIO I know not.

IAGO Is't possible?

CASSIO I remember a mass of things, but nothing distinctly; a quarrel, but nothing wherefore. O God, that
men should put an enemy in their mouths to steal away
their brains! that we should with joy, pleasance, revel,
280 and applause transform ourselves into beasts!

IAGO Why, but you are now well enough. How came you
thus recovered?

CASSIO It hath pleased the devil drunkenness to give
place to the devil wrath. One unperfectness shows me
another, to make me frankly despise myself.

IAGO Come, you are too severe a moraler. As the time, the
place, and the condition of this country stands, I could
heartily wish this had not so befall'n; but since it is as it
is, mend it for your own good.

CASSIO I will ask him for my place again: he shall tell me I
291 am a drunkard! Had I as many mouths as Hydra, such
an answer would stop them all. To be now a sensible
man, by and by a fool, and presently a beast! O strange!
294 Every inordinate cup is unblest, and the ingredient is a
devil.

IAGO Come, come, good wine is a good familiar creature
if it be well used. Exclaim no more against it. And, good

268 *parrot* meaningless phrases 269 *fustian* bombastic nonsense 280
applause desire to please 291 *Hydra* monster with many heads 294
ingredient contents

lieutenant, I think you think I love you.

CASSIO I have well approved it, sir. I drunk! 298

IAGO You or any man living may be drunk at some time,
man. I'll tell you what you shall do. Our general's wife is
now the general. I may say so in this respect, for that he
hath devoted and given up himself to the contemplation,
mark, and denotement of her parts and graces. Confess
yourself freely to her; importune her help to put you in
your place again. She is of so free, so kind, so apt, so 305
blessed a disposition she holds it a vice in her goodness
not to do more than she is requested. This broken joint
between you and her husband entreat her to splinter; 308
and my fortunes against any lay worth naming, this 309
crack of your love shall grow stronger than it was before.

CASSIO You advise me well.

IAGO I protest, in the sincerity of love and honest kind-
ness.

CASSIO I think it freely; and betimes in the morning will
I beseech the virtuous Desdemona to undertake for me.
I am desperate of my fortunes if they check me here.

IAGO You are in the right. Good night, lieutenant; I must
to the watch.

CASSIO Good night, honest Iago. *Exit Cassio.*

IAGO

And what's he then that says I play the villain,
When this advice is free I give and honest,
Probal to thinking, and indeed the course 321
To win the Moor again? For 'tis most easy
Th' inclining Desdemona to subdue 323
In any honest suit; she's framed as fruitful
As the free elements. And then for her
To win the Moor – were't to renounce his baptism,
All seals and symbols of redeemèd sin –
His soul is so enfettered to her love
That she may make, unmake, do what she list,

298 *approved* proved 305 *free* bounteous 308 *splinter* bind up with
splints 309 *lay* wager 321 *Probal* probable 323 *subdue* persuade

Even as her appetite shall play the god
With his weak function. How am I then a villain
332 To counsel Cassio to this parallel course,
333 Directly to his good? Divinity of hell!
334 When devils will the blackest sins put on,
They do suggest at first with heavenly shows,
As I do now. For whiles this honest fool
Plies Desdemona to repair his fortunes,
And she for him pleads strongly to the Moor,
I'll pour this pestilence into his ear,
340 That she repeals him for her body's lust;
And by how much she strives to do him good,
She shall undo her credit with the Moor.
So will I turn her virtue into pitch,
And out of her own goodness make the net
That shall enmesh them all.
          Enter Roderigo.   How, now, Roderigo?

RODERIGO I do follow here in the chase, not like a hound
347 that hunts, but one that fills up the cry. My money is almost spent; I have been to-night exceedingly well cudg-
elled; and I think the issue will be – I shall have so
much experience for my pains; and so, with no money
at all, and a little more wit, return again to Venice.

IAGO
How poor are they that have not patience!
What wound did ever heal but by degrees?
Thou know'st we work by wit, and not by witchcraft;
And wit depends on dilatory time.
Does't not go well? Cassio hath beaten thee,
357 And thou by that small hurt hast cashiered Cassio.
Though other things grow fair against the sun,
Yet fruits that blossom first will first be ripe.
Content thyself awhile. By the mass, 'tis morning!
Pleasure and action make the hours seem short.

332 *parallel* corresponding   333 *Divinity* theology   334 *put on* incite   340
repeals him seeks his recall   347 *cry* pack   357 *cashiered Cassio* maneuvered
Cassio's discharge

Retire thee; go where thou art billeted.
Away, I say! Thou shalt know more hereafter.
Nay, get thee gone!   *Exit Roderigo.*
            Two things are to be done:
My wife must move for Cassio to her mistress;
I'll set her on;
Myself the while to draw the Moor apart
And bring him jump when he may Cassio find   368
Soliciting his wife. Ay, that's the way!
Dull not device by coldness and delay.   *Exit.*

*

Enter Cassio, with Musicians and the Clown.   III, i

CASSIO
     Masters, play here, I will content your pains: 1
     Something that's brief; and bid 'Good morrow, general.'
     [They play.]

CLOWN Why, masters, ha' your instruments been in
     Naples, that they speak i' th' nose thus?   4

MUSICIAN How, sir, how?

CLOWN Are these, I pray you, called wind instruments?

MUSICIAN Ay, marry, are they, sir.

CLOWN O, thereby hangs a tail.

MUSICIAN Whereby hangs a tale, sir?

CLOWN Marry, sir, by many a wind instrument that I
     know. But, masters, here's money for you; and the
     general so likes your music that he desires you, for love's
     sake, to make no more noise with it.

MUSICIAN Well, sir, we will not.

CLOWN If you have any music that may not be heard, to't
     again: but, as they say, to hear music the general does
     not greatly care.

MUSICIAN We have none such, sir.

368 *jump* at the exact moment
III, i Before the chamber of Othello and Desdemona   1 *content* reward
4 *Naples* (notorious for its association with venereal disease)

CLOWN Then put up your pipes in your bag, for I'll away.
Go, vanish into air, away!

Exit Musician [with his fellows].

CASSIO Dost thou hear, my honest friend?

CLOWN No, I hear not your honest friend. I hear you.

23 CASSIO Prithee keep up thy quillets. There's a poor piece
of gold for thee. If the gentlewoman that attends the
general's wife be stirring, tell her there's one Cassio
entreats her a little favor of speech. Wilt thou do this?

CLOWN She is stirring sir. If she will stir hither, I shall
seem to notify unto her.

CASSIO

[Do, good my friend.]   *Exit Clown.*

29   *Enter Iago.*   In happy time, Iago.

IAGO

You have not been abed then?

CASSIO

Why, no; the day had broke
Before we parted. I have made bold, Iago,
To send in to your wife: my suit to her
Is that she will to virtuous Desdemona
Procure me some access.

IAGO   I'll send her to you presently;
And I'll devise a mean to draw the Moor
Out of the way, that your converse and business
May be more free.

CASSIO

I humbly thank you for't.   *Exit [Iago].*

I never knew

40   A Florentine more kind and honest.

Enter Emilia.

EMILIA

Good morrow, good lieutenant. I am sorry
For your displeasure; but all will sure be well.

---

23 *quillets* quips   29 *In happy time* well met   40 *Florentine* i.e. even a
Florentine (like Cassio; Iago was a Venetian)

The general and his wife are talking of it,
And she speaks for you stoutly. The Moor replies
That he you hurt is of great fame in Cyprus
And great affinity, and that in wholesome wisdom   46
He might not but refuse you; but he protests he loves
   you,
And needs no other suitor but his likings
[To take the safest occasion by the front]   49
To bring you in again.

CASSIO   Yet I beseech you,
If you think fit, or that it may be done,
Give me advantage of some brief discourse
With Desdemona alone.

EMILIA   Pray you come in.
I will bestow you where you shall have time
To speak your bosom freely.   55

CASSIO   I am much bound to you.
                                 Exeunt.

*

Enter Othello, Iago, and Gentlemen.   III, ii

OTHELLO
These letters give, Iago, to the pilot
And by him do my duties to the Senate.
That done, I will be walking on the works;   3
Repair there to me.

IAGO   Well, my good lord, I'll do't.

OTHELLO
This fortification, gentlemen, shall we see't?

GENTLEMEN
We'll wait upon your lordship.   *Exeunt.*

*

---

46 *affinity* family connections   49 *occasion* opportunity; *front* forelock   55
your bosom your inmost thoughts
III, ii The castle   3 *works* fortifications

III, iii   *Enter Desdemona, Cassio, and Emilia.*

DESDEMONA
Be thou assured, good Cassio, I will do
All my abilities in thy behalf.

EMILIA
Good madam, do. I warrant it grieves my husband
As if the cause were his.

DESDEMONA
O, that's an honest fellow. Do not doubt, Cassio,
But I will have my lord and you again
As friendly as you were.

CASSIO   Bounteous madam,
Whatever shall become of Michael Cassio,
He's never anything but your true servant.

DESDEMONA
I know't; I thank you. You do love my lord;
You have known him long; and be you well assured
12   He shall in strangeness stand no farther off
13   Than in a politic distance.

CASSIO   Ay, but, lady,
That policy may either last so long,
15   Or feed upon such nice and waterish diet,
Or breed itself so out of circumstance,
That, I being absent, and my place supplied,
My general will forget my love and service.

DESDEMONA
19   Do not doubt that; before Emilia here
I give thee warrant of thy place. Assure thee,
If I do vow a friendship, I'll perform it
To the last article. My lord shall never rest;
23   I'll watch him tame and talk him out of patience;
24   His bed shall seem a school, his board a shrift;

III, iii The castle grounds 12 *strangeness* aloofness 13 *Than . . . distance*
than wise policy requires 15 *Or . . . diet* or be continued for such slight
reasons 19 *doubt* fear 23 *watch him tame* keep him awake until he gives
in 24 *shrift* confessional

I'll intermingle everything he does
With Cassio's suit. Therefore be merry, Cassio,
For thy solicitor shall rather die
Than give thy cause away.
          Enter Othello and Iago [at a distance].

EMILIA
Madam, here comes my lord.

CASSIO
Madam, I'll take my leave.   30

DESDEMONA
Why, stay, and hear me speak.

CASSIO
Madam, not now : I am very ill at ease,
Unfit for mine own purposes.

DESDEMONA
Well, do your discretion.   *Exit Cassio.*

IAGO
Ha ! I like not that.

OTHELLO   What dost thou say ?

IAGO
Nothing, my lord ; or if – I know not what.

OTHELLO
Was not that Cassio parted from my wife ?

IAGO
Cassio, my lord ? No, sure, I cannot think it,
That he would steal away so guilty-like,
Seeing your coming.

OTHELLO   I do believe 'twas he.   40

DESDEMONA
How now, my lord ?
I have been talking with a suitor here,
A man that languishes in your displeasure.

OTHELLO
Who is't you mean ?

DESDEMONA
Why, your lieutenant, Cassio. Good my lord,
If I have any grace or power to move you,

47 His present reconciliation take;
    For if he be not one that truly loves you,
    That errs in ignorance, and not in cunning,
    I have no judgment in an honest face.
    I prithee call him back.

OTHELLO   Went he hence now?

DESDEMONA
    Yes, faith; so humbled
    That he hath left part of his grief with me
    To suffer with him. Good love, call him back.

OTHELLO
    Not now, sweet Desdemon; some other time.

DESDEMONA
    But shall't be shortly?

OTHELLO   The sooner, sweet, for you.

DESDEMONA
    Shall't be to-night at supper?

OTHELLO   No, not to-night.

DESDEMONA
    To-morrow dinner then?

OTHELLO   I shall not dine at home;
    I meet the captains at the citadel.

DESDEMONA
    Why then, to-morrow night, or Tuesday morn,
    On Tuesday noon or night, or Wednesday morn.
    I prithee name the time, but let it not
    Exceed three days. I' faith, he's penitent;
    And yet his trespass, in our common reason
    (Save that, they say, the wars must make examples
66 Out of their best), is not almost a fault
67 T' incur a private check. When shall he come?
    Tell me, Othello. I wonder in my soul
    What you could ask me that I should deny
70 Or stand so mamm'ring on. What? Michael Cassio,

---

47 *present* immediate   66 *not almost* hardly   67 *a private check* even a
private reprimand   70 *mamm'ring on* hesitating about

That came a-wooing with you, and so many a time,
When I have spoke of you dispraisingly,
Hath ta'en your part – to have so much to do
To bring him in ? By'r Lady, I could do much –

OTHELLO
Prithee no more. Let him come when he will !
I will deny thee nothing.

DESDEMONA   Why, this is not a boon ;
'Tis as I should entreat you wear your gloves,
Or feed on nourishing dishes, or keep you warm,
Or sue to you to do a peculiar profit
To your own person. Nay, when I have a suit
Wherein I mean to touch your love indeed,
It shall be full of poise and difficult weight,
And fearful to be granted.   83

OTHELLO   I will deny thee nothing !
Whereon I do beseech thee grant me this,
To leave me but a little to myself.

DESDEMONA
Shall I deny you ? No. Farewell, my lord.

OTHELLO
Farewell, my Desdemon : I'll come to thee straight.

DESDEMONA
Emilia, come. – Be as your fancies teach you ;
Whate'er you be, I am obedient.   *Exit [with Emilia]*

OTHELLO
Excellent wretch ! Perdition catch my soul   90
But I do love thee ! and when I love thee not,
Chaos is come again.

IAGO
My noble lord –

OTHELLO   What dost thou say, Iago ?

IAGO
Did Michael Cassio, when you wooed my lady,
Know of your love ?

83 *fearful* dangerous   90 *wretch* (a term of endearment)

83

OTHELLO
He did, from first to last. Why dost thou ask?

IAGO
But for a satisfaction of my thought;
No further harm.

OTHELLO   Why of thy thought, Iago?

IAGO
I did not think he had been acquainted with her.

OTHELLO
100 O, yes, and went between us very oft.

IAGO
Indeed?

OTHELLO
Indeed? Ay, indeed! Discern'st thou aught in that?
Is he not honest?

IAGO   Honest, my lord?

OTHELLO   Honest. Ay, honest.

IAGO
My lord, for aught I know.

OTHELLO
What dost thou think?

IAGO   Think, my lord?

OTHELLO   Think, my lord?
By heaven, he echoes me,
As if there were some monster in his thought
Too hideous to be shown. Thou dost mean something:
I heard thee say even now, thou lik'st not that,
When Cassio left my wife. What didst not like?
And when I told thee he was of my counsel
In my whole course of wooing, thou cried'st 'Indeed?'
And didst contract and purse thy brow together,
As if thou then hadst shut up in thy brain
115 Some horrible conceit. If thou dost love me,
Show me thy thought.

100 *went ... us* (i.e. as messenger)   115 *conceit* fancy

IAGO
　My lord, you know I love you.
OTHELLO　　　　　　　　　I think thou dost;
　And, for I know thou'rt full of love and honesty
　And weigh'st thy words before thou giv'st them breath,
　Therefore these stops of thine fright me the more;
　For such things in a false disloyal knave
　Are tricks of custom; but in a man that's just
　They are close dilations, working from the heart　　　123
　That passion cannot rule.
IAGO　　　　　　　　　For Michael Cassio,
　I dare be sworn I think that he is honest.
OTHELLO
　I think so too.
IAGO　　　　　Men should be what they seem;
　Or those that be not, would they might seem none!　　127
OTHELLO
　Certain, men should be what they seem.
IAGO
　Why then, I think Cassio's an honest man.
OTHELLO
　Nay, yet there's more in this.
　I prithee speak to me as to thy thinkings,
　As thou dost ruminate, and give thy worst of thoughts
　The worst of words.
IAGO　　　　　　　　Good my lord, pardon me:
　Though I am bound to every act of duty,
　I am not bound to that all slaves are free to.　　　　135
　Utter my thoughts? Why, say they are vile and false,
　As where's that palace whereinto foul things
　Sometimes intrude not? Who has a breast so pure
　But some uncleanly apprehensions

123-24 *close dilations . . . rule* secret emotions which well up in spite of
restraint　127 *seem none* i.e. not pretend to be men when they are really
monsters　135 *bound . . . free to* bound to tell that which even slaves are
allowed to keep to themselves

140   Keep leets and law days, and in Sessions sit
        With meditations lawful?

OTHELLO
   Thou dost conspire against thy friend, Iago,
   If thou but think'st him wronged, and mak'st his ear
   A stranger to thy thoughts.

IAGO   I do beseech you –
   Though I perchance am vicious in my guess
   (As I confess it is my nature's plague
147   To spy into abuses, and oft my jealousy
   Shapes faults that are not), that your wisdom yet
149   From one that so imperfectly conjects
   Would take no notice, nor build yourself a trouble
   Out of his scattering and unsure observance.
   It were not for your quiet nor your good,
   Nor for my manhood, honesty, and wisdom,
   To let you know my thoughts.

OTHELLO   What dost thou mean?

IAGO
   Good name in man and woman, dear my lord,
156   Is the immediate jewel of their souls.
   Who steals my purse steals trash; 'tis something,
        nothing;
   'Twas mine, 'tis his, and has been slave to thousands;
   But he that filches from me my good name
   Robs me of that which not enriches him
   And makes me poor indeed.

OTHELLO
   By heaven, I'll know thy thoughts!

IAGO
   You cannot, if my heart were in your hand;
   Nor shall not whilst 'tis in my custody.

OTHELLO
   Ha!

IAGO   O, beware, my lord, of jealousy!

---

140 *leets and law days* sittings of the courts   147 *jealousy* suspicion   149 *conjects* conjectures   156 *immediate* nearest the heart

It is the green-eyed monster, which doth mock   166
The meat it feeds on. That cuckold lives in bliss
Who, certain of his fate, loves not his wronger;
But O, what damnèd minutes tells he o'er
Who dotes, yet doubts – suspects, yet strongly loves!

OTHELLO
O misery!

IAGO
Poor and content is rich, and rich enough;
But riches fineless is as poor as winter   173
To him that ever fears he shall be poor.
Good God, the souls of all my tribe defend
From jealousy!

OTHELLO   Why, why is this?
Think'st thou I'ld make a life of jealousy,
To follow still the changes of the moon
With fresh suspicions? No! To be once in doubt
Is once to be resolved. Exchange me for a goat
When I shall turn the business of my soul
To such exsufflicate and blown surmises,   182
Matching this inference. 'Tis not to make me jealous
To say my wife is fair, feeds well, loves company,
Is free of speech, sings, plays, and dances;
Where virtue is, these are more virtuous.
Nor from mine own weak merits will I draw
The smallest fear or doubt of her revolt,   188
For she had eyes, and chose me. No, Iago;
I'll see before I doubt; when I doubt, prove;
And on the proof there is no more but this –
Away at once with love or jealousy!

IAGO
I am glad of this; for now I shall have reason
To show the love and duty that I bear you
With franker spirit. Therefore, as I am bound,
Receive it from me. I speak not yet of proof.

166 *mock* play with, like a cat with a mouse   173 *fineless* unlimited   182
exsufflicate and blown spat out and flyblown   188 *revolt* unfaithfulness

Look to your wife ; observe her well with Cassio ;
198   Wear your eyes thus, not jealous nor secure :
I would not have your free and noble nature,
200   Out of self-bounty, be abused. Look to't.
I know our country disposition well :
In Venice they do let God see the pranks
They dare not show their husbands ; their best
    conscience
Is not to leave't undone, but keep't unknown.

OTHELLO
Dost thou say so ?

IAGO
She did deceive her father, marrying you ;
And when she seemed to shake and fear your looks,
She loved them most.

OTHELLO   And so she did.

IAGO   Why, go to then !
She that, so young, could give out such a seeming
210   To seel her father's eyes up close as oak –
He thought 'twas witchcraft – but I am much to blame.
I humbly do beseech you of your pardon
For too much loving you.

OTHELLO   I am bound to thee for ever.

IAGO
I see this hath a little dashed your spirits.

OTHELLO
Not a jot, not a jot.

IAGO   I' faith, I fear it has.
I hope you will consider what is spoke
Comes from my love. But I do see y' are moved.
I am to pray you not to strain my speech
219   To grosser issues nor to larger reach
Than to suspicion.

OTHELLO
I will not.

---

198 *secure* overconfident   **200** *self-bounty* natural goodness   **210** *seel* close;
oak oak grain   **219** *To grosser issues* to mean something more monstrous

IAGO   Should you do so, my lord,
  My speech should fall into such vile success   222
  As my thoughts aim not at. Cassio's my worthy friend –
  My lord, I see y' are moved.

OTHELLO   No, not much moved :
  I do not think but Desdemona's honest.   225

IAGO

  Long live she so ! and long live you to think so !

OTHELLO

  And yet, how nature erring from itself –

IAGO

  Ay, there's the point ! as (to be bold with you)
  Not to affect many proposèd matches
  Of her own clime, complexion, and degree,
  Whereto we see in all things nature tends –
  Foh ! one may smell in such a will most rank,
  Foul disproportions, thoughts unnatural –
  But pardon me – I do not in position   234
  Distinctly speak of her ; though I may fear
  Her will, recoiling to her better judgment,   236
  May fall to match you with her country forms,   237
  And happily repent.   238

OTHELLO   Farewell, farewell !
  If more thou dost perceive, let me know more.
  Set on thy wife to observe. Leave me, Iago.

IAGO

  My lord, I take my leave.   *[Going.]*

OTHELLO

  Why did I marry ? This honest creature doubtless
  Sees and knows more, much more, than he unfolds.

IAGO *[returns]*

  My lord, I would I might entreat your honor
  To scan this thing no further : leave it to time.
  Although 'tis fit that Cassio have his place,

222 *vile success* evil outcome   225 *honest* chaste   234 *position* definite
assertion   236 *recoiling* reverting   237 *fall to match* happen to compare
238 *happily* haply, perhaps

For sure he fills it up with great ability,
Yet, if you please to hold him off awhile,
You shall by that perceive him and his means.
250 Note if your lady strain his entertainment
With any strong or vehement importunity;
Much will be seen in that. In the mean time
253 Let me be thought too busy in my fears
(As worthy cause I have to fear I am)
255 And hold her free, I do beseech your honor.

OTHELLO
256 Fear not my government.

IAGO
I once more take my leave.   *Exit.*

OTHELLO
This fellow's of exceeding honesty,
259 And knows all qualities, with a learned spirit
260 Of human dealings. If I do prove her haggard,
261 Though that her jesses were my dear heartstrings,
262 I'd whistle her off and let her down the wind
To prey at fortune. Haply, for I am black
264 And have not those soft parts of conversation
265 That chamberers have, or for I am declined
Into the vale of years – yet that's not much –
She's gone. I am abused, and my relief
Must be to loathe her. O curse of marriage,
That we can call these delicate creatures ours,
And not their appetites! I had rather be a toad
And live upon the vapor of a dungeon
Than keep a corner in the thing I love
273 For others' uses. Yet 'tis the plague of great ones;
274 Prerogatived are they less than the base.

---

250 *strain his entertainment* urge his recall   **253** *busy* meddlesome   **255** *hold her free* consider her guiltless   **256** *government* self-control   **259** *qualities* natures   **259–60** *learned spirit Of* mind informed about   **260** *haggard* a wild hawk   **261** *jesses* thongs for controlling a hawk   **262–63** *whistle . . . fortune* turn her out and let her take care of herself   **264** *soft . . . conversation* ingratiating manners   **265** *chamberers* courtiers   **273** *great ones* prominent men   **274** *Prerogatived* privileged

'Tis destiny unshunnable, like death.
Even then this forkèd plague is fated to us   276
When we do quicken. Look where she comes.   277
      Enter Desdemona and Emilia.
If she be false, O, then heaven mocks itself!
I'll not believe't.

DESDEMONA   How now, my dear Othello?
Your dinner, and the generous islanders   280
By you invited, do attend your presence.

OTHELLO
I am to blame.

DESDEMONA   Why do you speak so faintly?
Are you not well?

OTHELLO
I have a pain upon my forehead, here.

DESDEMONA
Faith, that's with watching; 'twill away again.   285
Let me but bind it hard, within this hour
It will be well.

OTHELLO   Your napkin is too little;   287
    [He pushes the handkerchief from him, and it falls
    unnoticed.]
Let it alone. Come, I'll go in with you.   288

DESDEMONA
I am very sorry that you are not well. *Exit [with Othello].*

EMILIA
I am glad I have found this napkin;
This was her first remembrance from the Moor,
My wayward husband hath a hundred times
Wooed me to steal it; but she so loves the token
(For he conjured her she should ever keep it)
That she reserves it evermore about her
To kiss and talk to. I'll have the work ta'en out   296
And give't Iago.

276 *forkèd plague* i.e. horns of a cuckold 277 *do quicken* are born 280
generous noble 285 *watching* working late 287 *napkin* handkerchief 288
it i.e. his forehead 296 *work ta'en out* pattern copied

What he will do with it heaven knows, not I;
299 I nothing but to please his fantasy.
                Enter Iago.

IAGO
How now? What do you here alone?

EMILIA
Do not you chide; I have a thing for you.

IAGO
A thing for me? It is a common thing—

EMILIA Ha?

IAGO
To have a foolish wife.

EMILIA
O, is that all? What will you give me now
For that same handkerchief?

IAGO   What handkerchief?

EMILIA
What handkerchief!
Why, that the Moor first gave to Desdemona;
That which so often you did bid me steal.

IAGO
Hast stol'n it from her?

EMILIA
No, faith; she let it drop by negligence,
312 And to th' advantage, I, being here, took't up.
Look, here it is.

IAGO   A good wench! Give it me.

EMILIA
What will you do with't, that you have been so earnest
To have me filch it?

IAGO   Why, what is that to you?
      [Snatches it.]

EMILIA
316 If it be not for some purpose of import,
Give't me again. Poor lady, she'll run mad

299 *fantasy* whim   **312** *to th' advantage* opportunely   **316** *import* impor-
tance

When she shall lack it.

IAGO

Be not acknown on't ; I have use for it.   319
Go, leave me.   *Exit Emilia.*
I will in Cassio's lodgings lose this napkin
And let him find it. Trifles light as air
Are to the jealous confirmations strong
As proofs of holy writ. This may do something.
The Moor already changes with my poison :
Dangerous conceits are in their natures poisons,   326
Which at the first are scarce found to distaste,
But with a little act upon the blood
Burn like the mines of sulphur.
       Enter Othello.   I did say so.
Look where he comes ! Not poppy nor mandragora,   330
Nor all the drowsy syrups of the world,
Shall ever med'cine thee to that sweet sleep
Which thou owedst yesterday.

OTHELLO   Ha ! ha ! false to me ?

IAGO

Why, how now, general ? No more of that !

OTHELLO

Avaunt ! be gone ! Thou hast set me on the rack.
I swear 'tis better to be much abused
Than but to know't a little.

IAGO   How now, my lord ?

OTHELLO

What sense had I of her stol'n hours of lust ?
I saw't not, thought it not, it harmed not me ;
I slept the next night well, fed well, was free and merry ;   340
I found not Cassio's kisses on her lips.
He that is robbed, not wanting what is stol'n,   342
Let him not know't, and he's not robbed at all.

IAGO

I am sorry to hear this.

319 *Be . . . on't* do not acknowledge it   326 *conceits* ideas   330 *mandragora*
a narcotic   340 *free* carefree   342 *wanting* missing

OTHELLO
I had been happy if the general camp,
346   Pioners and all, had tasted her sweet body,
So I had nothing known. O, now for ever
Farewell the tranquil mind! farewell content!
349   Farewell the plumèd troop, and the big wars
That make ambition virtue! O, farewell!
Farewell the neighing steed and the shrill trump,
The spirit-stirring drum, th' ear-piercing fife,
The royal banner, and all quality,
354   Pride, pomp, and circumstance of glorious war!
355   And O you mortal engines whose rude throats
356   Th' immortal Jove's dread clamors counterfeit,
Farewell! Othello's occupation's gone!

IAGO
Is't possible, my lord?

OTHELLO
Villain, be sure thou prove my love a whore!
Be sure of it; give me the ocular proof;
Or, by the worth of mine eternal soul,
Thou hadst been better have been born a dog
Than answer my waked wrath!

IAGO   Is't come to this?

OTHELLO
Make me to see't; or at the least so prove it
365   That the probation bear no hinge nor loop
To hang a doubt on – or woe upon thy life!

IAGO
My noble lord –

OTHELLO
If thou dost slander her and torture me,
Never pray more; abandon all remorse;
On horror's head horrors accumulate;
Do deeds to make heaven weep, all earth amazed;

---

346 *Pioners* sappers, laborers   349 *big* stately   354 *circumstance* pageantry
355 *mortal engines* deadly artillery   356 *counterfeit* imitate   365 *probation* proof

For nothing canst thou to damnation add
Greater than that.

IAGO   O grace! O heaven forgive me!
Are you a man? Have you a soul or sense? –
God b' wi' you! take mine office. O wretched fool,
That liv'st to make thine honesty a vice!
O monstrous world! Take note, take note, O world,
To be direct and honest is not safe.
I thank you for this profit; and from hence   379
I'll love no friend, sith love breeds such offense.

OTHELLO
Nay, stay. Thou shouldst be honest.

IAGO
I should be wise; for honesty's a fool
And loses that it works for.

OTHELLO   By the world,
I think my wife be honest, and think she is not;
I think that thou art just, and think thou art not.
I'll have some proof. Her name, that was as fresh
As Dian's visage, is now begrimed and black
As mine own face. If there be cords, or knives,
Poison, or fire, or suffocating streams,
I'll not endure it. Would I were satisfied!   390

IAGO
I see, sir, you are eaten up with passion:
I do repent me that I put it to you.
You would be satisfied?

OTHELLO   Would? Nay, I will.

IAGO
And may; but how? how satisfied, my lord?
Would you, the supervisor, grossly gape on?   395
Behold her topped?

OTHELLO   Death and damnation! O!

IAGO
It were a tedious difficulty, I think,

379 *profit* profitable lesson   390 *satisfied* completely informed   395 *supervisor* spectator

95

To bring them to that prospect. Damn them then,
399 If ever mortal eyes do see them bolster
More than their own! What then? How then?
What shall I say? Where's satisfaction?
It is impossible you should see this,
403 Were they as prime as goats, as hot as monkeys,
404 As salt as wolves in pride, and fools as gross
As ignorance made drunk. But yet, I say,
If imputation and strong circumstances
Which lead directly to the door of truth
Will give you satisfaction, you may have't.

OTHELLO
Give me a living reason she's disloyal.

IAGO
410 I do not like the office.
But sith I am ent'red in this cause so far,
Pricked to't by foolish honesty and love,
I will go on. I lay with Cassio lately,
And being troubled with a raging tooth,
I could not sleep.
There are a kind of men so loose of soul
That in their sleeps will mutter their affairs.
One of this kind is Cassio.
In sleep I heard him say, 'Sweet Desdemona,
420 Let us be wary, let us hide our loves!'
And then, sir, would he gripe and wring my hand,
Cry 'O sweet creature!' and then kiss me hard,
As if he plucked up kisses by the roots
That grew upon my lips; then laid his leg
Over my thigh, and sighed, and kissed, and then
Cried 'Cursèd fate that gave thee to the Moor!'

OTHELLO
O monstrous! monstrous!

IAGO   Nay, this was but his dream.

---

399 *bolster* lie together   403 *prime* lustful   404 *salt* lecherous; *pride*
heat

OTHELLO

But this denoted a foregone conclusion :   428
'Tis a shrewd doubt, though it be but a dream.   429

IAGO

And this may help to thicken other proofs
That do demonstrate thinly.

OTHELLO   I'll tear her all to pieces !

IAGO

Nay, but be wise. Yet we see nothing done ;
She may be honest yet. Tell me but this –
Have you not sometimes seen a handkerchief
Spotted with strawberries in your wife's hand ?

OTHELLO

I gave her such a one ; 'twas my first gift.

IAGO

I know not that ; but such a handkerchief –
I am sure it was your wife's – did I to-day
See Cassio wipe his beard with.

OTHELLO   If it be that –

IAGO

If it be that, or any that was hers,   440
It speaks against her with the other proofs.

OTHELLO

O, that the slave had forty thousand lives !
One is too poor, too weak for my revenge.
Now do I see 'tis true. Look here, Iago :
All my fond love thus do I blow to heaven.
'Tis gone.
Arise, black vengeance, from the hollow hell !
Yield up, O love, thy crown and hearted throne
To tyrannous hate ! Swell, bosom, with thy fraught,   449
For 'tis of aspics' tongues !   450

IAGO   Yet be content.

OTHELLO

O, blood, blood, blood !

428 *foregone conclusion* previous experience   429 *a shrewd doubt* cursedly
suspicious   449 *fraught* burden   450 *aspics* deadly poisonous snakes

IAGO
    Patience, I say. Your mind perhaps may change.

OTHELLO
453   Never, Iago. Like to the Pontic sea,
    Whose icy current and compulsive course
    Ne'er feels retiring ebb, but keeps due on
    To the Propontic and the Hellespont,
    Even so my bloody thoughts, with violent pace,
    Shall ne'er look back, ne'er ebb to humble love,
459   Till that a capable and wide revenge
    Swallow them up.
            He kneels.   Now, by yond marble heaven,
    In the due reverence of a sacred vow
    I here engage my words.

IAGO   Do not rise yet.
    Iago kneels.
    Witness, you ever-burning lights above,
464   You elements that clip us round about,
    Witness that here Iago doth give up
466   The execution of his wit, hands, heart
    To wronged Othello's service ! Let him command,
468   And to obey shall be in me remorse,
    What bloody business ever.
        [*They rise.*]

OTHELLO   I greet thy love,
    Not with vain thanks but with acceptance bounteous,
    And will upon the instant put thee to't.
    Within these three days let me hear thee say
    That Cassio's not alive.

IAGO
    My friend is dead ; 'tis done at your request.
    But let her live.

OTHELLO
    Damn her, lewd minx ! O, damn her ! damn her !

---

453 *Pontic sea* Black Sea   459 *capable* all-embracing   464 *clip* encompass
466 *execution* activities ; *wit* mind   468 *remorse* pity

Come, go with me apart. I will withdraw
To furnish me with some swift means of death
For the fair devil. Now art thou my lieutenant.

IAGO

I am your own for ever.   *Exeunt.*

*

Enter Desdemona, Emilia, and Clown.   III, iv

DESDEMONA Do you know, sirrah, where Lieutenant
Cassio lies ?   2

CLOWN I dare not say he lies anywhere.

DESDEMONA Why, man ?

CLOWN He's a soldier, and for me to say a soldier lies is
stabbing.

DESDEMONA Go to. Where lodges he ?

CLOWN To tell you where he lodges is to tell you where I
lie.

DESDEMONA Can anything be made of this ?

CLOWN I know not where he lodges ; and for me to devise
a lodging, and say he lies here or he lies there, were to
lie in mine own throat.

DESDEMONA Can you enquire him out, and be edified by
report ?

CLOWN I will catechize the world for him ; that is, make
questions, and by them answer.

DESDEMONA Seek him, bid him come hither. Tell him I
have moved my lord on his behalf and hope all will be   19
well.

CLOWN To do this is within the compass of man's wit,
and therefore I'll attempt the doing of it.   *Exit.*

DESDEMONA

Where should I lose that handkerchief, Emilia ?

EMILIA

I know not, madam.

III, iv The environs of the castle   2 *lies* lives, lodges   19 *moved* made
proposals

DESDEMONA

Believe me, I had rather have lost my purse
26   Full of crusadoes; and but my noble Moor
Is true of mind, and made of no such baseness
As jealous creatures are, it were enough
To put him to ill thinking.

EMILIA   Is he not jealous?

DESDEMONA

Who? he? I think the sun where he was born
31   Drew all such humors from him.
        Enter Othello.

EMILIA   Look where he comes.

DESDEMONA

I will not leave him now till Cassio
Be called to him. – How is't with you, my lord?

OTHELLO

Well, my good lady. *[aside]* O, hardness to dissemble! –
How do you, Desdemona?

DESDEMONA   Well, my good lord.

OTHELLO

Give me your hand. This hand is moist, my lady.

DESDEMONA

It yet hath felt no age nor known no sorrow.

OTHELLO

This argues fruitfulness and liberal heart.
Hot, hot, and moist. This hand of yours requires
40   A sequester from liberty, fasting and prayer,
Much castigation, exercise devout;
For here's a young and sweating devil here
That commonly rebels. 'Tis a good hand,
A frank one.

DESDEMONA You may, indeed, say so;
For 'twas that hand that gave away my heart.

OTHELLO

A liberal hand! The hearts of old gave hands;

26 *crusadoes* Portuguese gold coins   31 *humors* inclinations   40 *sequester*
removal

But our new heraldry is hands, not hearts.   47

DESDEMONA
I cannot speak of this. Come now, your promise!

OTHELLO
What promise, chuck?

DESDEMONA
I have sent to bid Cassio come speak with you.

OTHELLO
I have a salt and sorry rheum offends me.   51
Lend me thy handkerchief.

DESDEMONA   Here, my lord.

OTHELLO
That which I gave you.

DESDEMONA   I have it not about me.

OTHELLO
Not?

DESDEMONA No, faith, my lord.

OTHELLO   That's a fault.
That handkerchief
Did an Egyptian to my mother give.   56
She was a charmer, and could almost read   57
The thoughts of people. She told her, while she kept it,
'Twould make her amiable and subdue my father   59
Entirely to her love; but if she lost it
Or made a gift of it, my father's eye
Should hold her loathèd, and his spirits should hunt
After new fancies. She, dying, gave it me,
And bid me, when my fate would have me wive,
To give it her. I did so; and take heed on't;
Make it a darling like your precious eye.
To lose't or give't away were such perdition   67
As nothing else could match.

DESDEMONA   Is't possible?

---

47 *heraldry* heraldic symbolism   51 *salt . . . rheum* distressing head-cold
56 *Egyptian* gypsy   57 *charmer* sorceress   59 *amiable* lovable   67 *perdition*
disaster

OTHELLO
'Tis true. There's magic in the web of it.
A sibyl that had numb'red in the world
71   The sun to course two hundred compasses,
In her prophetic fury sewed the work;
The worms were hallowed that did breed the silk;
74   And it was dyed in mummy which the skillful
Conserved of maidens' hearts.

DESDEMONA   I' faith? Is't true?

OTHELLO
Most veritable. Therefore look to't well.

DESDEMONA
Then would to God that I had never seen't!

OTHELLO Ha! Wherefore?

DESDEMONA
Why do you speak so startingly and rash?

OTHELLO
Is't lost? Is't gone? Speak, is it out o' th' way?

DESDEMONA Heaven bless us!

OTHELLO Say you?

DESDEMONA
It is not lost. But what an if it were?

OTHELLO How?

DESDEMONA
I say it is not lost.

OTHELLO   Fetch't, let me see't!

DESDEMONA
Why, so I can, sir; but I will not now.
87   This is a trick to put me from my suit:
Pray you let Cassio be received again.

OTHELLO
Fetch me the handkerchief! My mind misgives.

DESDEMONA
Come, come!
You'll never meet a more sufficient man.

---

71 *compasses* annual rounds   74 *mummy* a drug made from mummies   87 *put* divert

OTHELLO
The handkerchief!

[DESDEMONA   I pray talk me of Cassio.

OTHELLO
The handkerchief!]

DESDEMONA   A man that all his time   93
Hath founded his good fortunes on your love,
Shared dangers with you –

OTHELLO
The handkerchief!

DESDEMONA
I' faith, you are to blame.

OTHELLO Zounds!   *Exit Othello.*

EMILIA Is not this man jealous?

DESDEMONA
I ne'er saw this before.
Sure there's some wonder in this handkerchief;
I am most unhappy in the loss of it.

EMILIA
'Tis not a year or two shows us a man.
They are all but stomachs, and we all but food;
They eat us hungerly, and when they are full,
They belch us.
          Enter Iago and Cassio.
                    Look you – Cassio and my husband!

IAGO
There is no other way; 'tis she must do't.
And lo the happiness! Go and importune her.   108

DESDEMONA
How now, good Cassio? What's the news with you?

CASSIO
Madam, my former suit. I do beseech you
That by your virtuous means I may again
Exist, and be a member of his love
Whom I with all the office of my heart

93 *all . . . time* during his whole career   108 *happiness* good luck

Entirely honor. I would not be delayed.
If my offense be of such mortal kind
That neither service past, nor present sorrows,
Nor purposed merit in futurity,
Can ransom me into his love again,
But to know so must be my benefit.
So shall I clothe me in a forced content,
121   And shut myself up in some other course,
To fortune's alms.

DESDEMONA   Alas, thrice-gentle Cassio!
123   My advocation is not now in tune.
My lord is not my lord; nor should I know him,
125   Were he in favor as in humor altered.
So help me every spirit sanctified
As I have spoken for you all my best
128   And stood within the blank of his displeasure
For my free speech! You must awhile be patient.
What I can do I will; and more I will
Than for myself I dare. Let that suffice you.

IAGO
Is my lord angry?

EMILIA   He went hence but now,
And certainly in strange unquietness.

IAGO
Can he be angry? I have seen the cannon
When it hath blown his ranks into the air
And, like the devil, from his very arm
Puffed his own brother – and is he angry?
Something of moment then. I will go meet him.
There's matter in't indeed if he be angry.

DESDEMONA
I prithee do so.   *Exit [Iago].*
140   Something sure of state,
141   Either from Venice or some unhatched practice

---

121 *shut myself up in* confine myself to   123 *advocation* advocacy   125 *favor* appearance   128 *blank* bull's-eye of the target   140 *state* public affairs 141 *unhatched practice* budding plot

Made demonstrable here in Cyprus to him,
Hath puddled his clear spirit; and in such cases   143
Men's natures wrangle with inferior things,
Though great ones are their object. 'Tis even so;
For let our finger ache, and it endues   146
Our other, healthful members even to a sense
Of pain. Nay, we must think men are not gods,
Nor of them look for such observancy
As fits the bridal. Beshrew me much, Emilia,
I was, unhandsome warrior as I am,   151
Arraigning his unkindness with my soul;   152
But now I find I had suborned the witness,
And he's indicted falsely.

EMILIA
Pray heaven it be state matters, as you think,
And no conception nor no jealous toy   156
Concerning you.

DESDEMONA
Alas the day! I never gave him cause.

EMILIA
But jealous souls will not be answered so;
They are not ever jealous for the cause,
But jealous for they're jealous. 'Tis a monster
Begot upon itself, born on itself.   162

DESDEMONA
Heaven keep that monster from Othello's mind!

EMILIA Lady, amen.

DESDEMONA
I will go seek him. Cassio, walk here about:
If I do find him fit, I'll move your suit
And seek to effect it to my uttermost.

CASSIO
I humbly thank your ladyship.
                    Exeunt Desdemona and Emilia.

---

143 *puddled* muddied   146 *endues* brings   151 *unhandsome warrior* in-
adequate soldier   152 *Arraigning . . . soul* indicting his unkindness before
the bar of my soul   156 *toy* fancy   162 *Begot . . . itself* self-engendered

Enter Bianca.

BIANCA
Save you, friend Cassio!

CASSIO   What make you from home?
How is't with you, my most fair Bianca?
I' faith, sweet love, I was coming to your house.

BIANCA
And I was going to your lodging, Cassio.
What, keep a week away? seven days and nights?
Eightscore eight hours? and lovers' absent hours,
175   More tedious than the dial eightscore times?
O weary reck'ning!

CASSIO   Pardon me, Bianca:
I have this while with leaden thoughts been pressed;
178   But I shall in a more continuate time
Strike off this score of absence. Sweet Bianca,
       [Gives her Desdemona's handkerchief.]
180   Take me this work out.

BIANCA   O Cassio, whence came this?
This is some token from a newer friend.
To the felt absence now I feel a cause.
Is't come to this? Well, well.

CASSIO   Go to, woman!
Throw your vile guesses in the devil's teeth,
From whence you have them. You are jealous now
That this is from some mistress, some remembrance.
No, by my faith, Bianca.

BIANCA   Why, whose is it?

CASSIO
I know not, sweet; I found it in my chamber.
189   I like the work well; ere it be demanded,
As like enough it will, I'd have it copied.
Take it and do't, and leave me for this time.

BIANCA
Leave you? Wherefore?

175 *dial* clock   178 *continuate* uninterrupted   180 *Take . . . out* copy this
embroidery for me   189 *work* needlework

CASSIO
I do attend here on the general
And think it no addition, nor my wish,
To have him see me womaned.

BIANCA   Why, I pray you ?

CASSIO
Not that I love you not.

BIANCA   But that you do not love me !
I pray you bring me on the way a little,
And say if I shall see you soon at night.

CASSIO
'Tis but a little way that I can bring you,
For I attend here ; but I'll see you soon.

BIANCA
'Tis very good. I must be circumstanced.   *Exeunt.* 201

*

Enter Othello and Iago.   IV, i

IAGO
Will you think so ?

OTHELLO   Think so, Iago ?

IAGO   What,
To kiss in private ?

OTHELLO   An unauthorized kiss.

IAGO
Or to be naked with her friend in bed
An hour or more, not meaning any harm ?

OTHELLO
Naked in bed, Iago, and not mean harm ?
It is hypocrisy against the devil.   6
They that mean virtuously, and yet do so,
The devil their virtue tempts, and they tempt heaven.

IAGO
So they do nothing, 'tis a venial slip.

---

201 *circumstanced* governed by circumstances
IV, i The environs of the castle   6 *hypocrisy . . . devil* i.e. feigned sin
instead of feigned virtue

But if I give my wife a handkerchief –

OTHELLO
What then?

IAGO
Why, then 'tis hers, my lord; and being hers,
She may, I think, bestow't on any man.

OTHELLO
She is protectress of her honor too;
May she give that?

IAGO
Her honor is an essence that's not seen;
They have it very oft that have it not.
But for the handkerchief –

OTHELLO
By heaven, I would most gladly have forgot it!
Thou said'st – O, it comes o'er my memory
21   As doth the raven o'er the infected house,
Boding to all! – he had my handkerchief.

IAGO
Ay, what of that?

OTHELLO   That's not so good now.

IAGO   What
If I had said I had seen him do you wrong?
Or heard him say – as knaves be such abroad
Who having, by their own importunate suit,
Or voluntary dotage of some mistress,
28   Convincèd or supplied them, cannot choose
But they must blab –

OTHELLO   Hath he said anything?

IAGO
He hath, my lord; but be you well assured,
No more than he'll unswear.

OTHELLO   What hath he said?

IAGO
Faith, that he did – I know not what he did.

---

21 *infected* plague-stricken 28 *Convincèd or supplied* overcome or gratified

OTHELLO What? what?

IAGO
  Lie –

OTHELLO With her?

IAGO   With her, on her; what you will.

OTHELLO Lie with her? lie on her? – We say lie on her
  when they belie her. – Lie with her! Zounds, that's ful-
  some. – Handkerchief – confessions – handkerchief! –
  To confess, and be hanged for his labor – first to be
  hanged, and then to confess! I tremble at it. Nature 39
  would not invest herself in such shadowing passion
  without some instruction. It is not words that shakes me
  thus. – Pish! Noses, ears, and lips? Is't possible? – Confess? – Handkerchief? – O devil!
     Falls in a trance.

IAGO Work on,
  My med'cine, work! Thus credulous fools are caught,
  And many worthy and chaste dames even thus,
  All guiltless, meet reproach. – What, ho! my lord!
  My lord, I say! Othello!
     Enter Cassio.   How now, Cassio?

CASSIO
  What's the matter?

IAGO
  My lord is fall'n into an epilepsy.
  This is his second fit; he had one yesterday.

CASSIO
  Rub him about the temples.

IAGO   No, forbear.
  The lethargy must have his quiet course.   53
  If not, he foams at mouth, and by and by
  Breaks out to savage madness. Look, he stirs.
  Do you withdraw yourself a little while.
  He will recover straight. When he is gone,
  I would on great occasion speak with you. *[Exit Cassio.]*

39–41 *Nature ... instruction* my natural faculties would not be so overcome
by passion without reason   **53** *lethargy* coma

How is it, general ? Have you not hurt your head ?

OTHELLO
Dost thou mock me ?

IAGO   I mock you ? No, by heaven.
Would you would bear your fortune like a man !

OTHELLO
62 A hornèd man 's a monster and a beast.

IAGO
There's many a beast then in a populous city,
And many a civil monster.

OTHELLO
Did he confess it ?

IAGO   Good sir, be a man.
Think every bearded fellow that's but yoked
May draw with you. There's millions now alive
68 That nightly lie in those unproper beds
69 Which they dare swear peculiar : your case is better.
O, 'tis the spite of hell, the fiend's arch-mock,
71 To lip a wanton in a secure couch,
And to suppose her chaste ! No, let me know ;
And knowing what I am, I know what she shall be.

OTHELLO
O, thou art wise ! 'Tis certain.

IAGO   Stand you awhile apart ;
75 Confine yourself but in a patient list.
Whilst you were here, o'erwhelmèd with your grief –
A passion most unsuiting such a man –
Cassio came hither. I shifted him away
79 And laid good 'scuse upon your ecstasy ;
Bade him anon return, and here speak with me ;
81 The which he promised. Do but encave yourself
And mark the fleers, the gibes, and notable scorns
That dwell in every region of his face ;

62 *hornèd man* cuckold 68 *unproper* not exclusively their own 69
peculiar exclusively their own 71 *secure* free from fear of rivalry 75 *in a
patient list* within the limits of self-control 79 *ecstasy* trance 81 *encave*
conceal

For I will make him tell the tale anew –
Where, how, how oft, how long ago, and when
He hath, and is again to cope your wife.   86
I say, but mark his gesture. Marry, patience!
Or I shall say y'are all in all in spleen,   88
And nothing of a man.
OTHELLO   Dost thou hear, Iago?
I will be found most cunning in my patience;
But – dost thou hear? – most bloody.
IAGO   That's not amiss;
But yet keep time in all. Will you withdraw?
                              [*Othello retires.*]
Now will I question Cassio of Bianca,
A huswife that by selling her desires   94
Buys herself bread and clothes. It is a creature
That dotes on Cassio, as 'tis the strumpet's plague
To beguile many and be beguiled by one.
He, when he hears of her, cannot refrain
From the excess of laughter. Here he comes.
      Enter Cassio.
As he shall smile, Othello shall go mad;
And his unbookish jealousy must conster   101
Poor Cassio's smiles, gestures, and light behavior
Quite in the wrong. How do you now, lieutenant?
CASSIO
The worser that you give me the addition   104
Whose want even kills me.
IAGO
Ply Desdemona well, and you are sure on't.
Now, if this suit lay in Bianca's power,
How quickly should you speed!
CASSIO   Alas, poor caitiff!   108
OTHELLO
Look how he laughs already!

---

86 *cope* meet 88 *all in all in spleen* wholly overcome by your passion 94
huswife hussy 101 *unbookish* uninstructed; *conster* construe, interpret
104 *addition* title 108 *caitiff* wretch

IAGO

I never knew a woman love man so.

CASSIO

Alas, poor rogue! I think, i' faith, she loves me.

OTHELLO

Now he denies it faintly, and laughs it out.

IAGO

Do you hear, Cassio?

OTHELLO   Now he importunes him

To tell it o'er. Go to! Well said, well said!

IAGO

She gives it out that you shall marry her.

Do you intend it?

CASSIO Ha, ha, ha!

OTHELLO

Do you triumph, Roman? Do you triumph?

119 CASSIO I marry her? What, a customer? Prithee bear

some charity to my wit; do not think it so unwholesome.

Ha, ha, ha!

OTHELLO So, so, so, so! They laugh that win!

IAGO

Faith, the cry goes that you shall marry her.

CASSIO Prithee say true.

IAGO I am a very villain else.

126 OTHELLO Have you scored me? Well.

CASSIO This is the monkey's own giving out. She is per-

suaded I will marry her out of her own love and flattery,

not out of my promise.

130 OTHELLO Iago beckons me; now he begins the story.

CASSIO She was here even now; she haunts me in every

place. I was t' other day talking on the sea bank with cer-

133 tain Venetians, and thither comes the bauble, and, by

this hand, she falls me thus about my neck –

OTHELLO Crying 'O dear Cassio!' as it were. His gesture

imports it.

119 *customer* prostitute   126 *scored me* settled my account (?)   130 *beckons*
signals   133 *bauble* plaything

CASSIO So hangs, and lolls, and weeps upon me; so shakes and pulls me! Ha, ha, ha!

OTHELLO Now he tells how she plucked him to my chamber. O, I see that nose of yours, but not that dog I shall throw it to.

CASSIO Well, I must leave her company.

Enter Bianca.

IAGO Before me! Look where she comes.

CASSIO 'Tis such another fitchew! marry, a perfumed 144 one. What do you mean by this haunting of me?

BIANCA Let the devil and his dam haunt you! What did you mean by that same handkerchief you gave me even now? I was a fine fool to take it. I must take out the whole work? A likely piece of work that you should find it in your chamber and know not who left it there! This is some minx's token, and I must take out the work? There! Give it your hobby-horse. Wheresoever you had 152 it, I'll take out no work on't.

CASSIO How now, my sweet Bianca? How now? how now?

OTHELLO By heaven, that should be my handkerchief!

BIANCA An you'll come to supper to-night, you may; an you will not, come when you are next prepared for. *Exit.*

IAGO After her, after her!

CASSIO Faith, I must; she'll rail in the street else.

IAGO Will you sup there?

CASSIO Yes, I intend so.

IAGO Well, I may chance to see you; for I would very fain speak with you.

CASSIO Prithee come. Will you?

IAGO Go to! say no more.   *Exit Cassio.*

OTHELLO *[comes forward]* How shall I murder him, Iago?

IAGO Did you perceive how he laughed at his vice? 168

OTHELLO O Iago!

IAGO And did you see the handkerchief?

144 *fitchew* polecat (slang for whore)   152 *hobby-horse* harlot   168 *vice* i.e. vicious conduct

OTHELLO Was that mine?

172 IAGO Yours, by this hand! And to see how he prizes the foolish woman your wife! She gave it him, and he hath giv'n it his whore.

OTHELLO I would have him nine years a-killing! – A fine woman! a fair woman! a sweet woman!

IAGO Nay, you must forget that.

OTHELLO Ay, let her rot, and perish, and be damned tonight; for she shall not live. No, my heart is turned to stone; I strike it, and it hurts my hand. O, the world hath not a sweeter creature! She might lie by an emperor's side and command him tasks.

IAGO Nay, that's not your way.

OTHELLO Hang her! I do but say what she is. So delicate with her needle! an admirable musician! O, she will sing the savageness out of a bear! Of so high and plente-
187 ous wit and invention –

IAGO She's the worse for all this.

OTHELLO O, a thousand thousand times! And then, of so
190 gentle a condition!

IAGO Ay, too gentle.

OTHELLO Nay, that's certain. But yet the pity of it, Iago! O Iago, the pity of it, Iago!

194 IAGO If you are so fond over her iniquity, give her patent to offend; for if it touch not you, it comes near nobody.

OTHELLO I will chop her into messes! Cuckold me!

IAGO O, 'tis foul in her.

OTHELLO With mine officer!

IAGO That's fouler.

OTHELLO Get me some poison, Iago, this night. I'll not
201 expostulate with her, lest her body and beauty un-provide my mind again. This night, Iago!

IAGO Do it not with poison. Strangle her in her bed, even the bed she hath contaminated.

---

172 *prizes* values   187 *invention* imagination   190 *condition* disposition
194 *patent* license   201 *unprovide* disarm

OTHELLO Good, good! The justice of it pleases. Very
    good!

IAGO And for Cassio, let me be his undertaker: you shall 206
    hear more by midnight.

OTHELLO
Excellent good!
       A trumpet. What trumpet is that same?

IAGO
I warrant something from Venice.
      Enter Lodovico, Desdemona, and Attendants.
                    'Tis Lodovico.
This comes from the Duke; and see, your wife is with 210
    him.

LODOVICO
God save you, worthy general!

OTHELLO   With all my heart, sir.

LODOVICO
The Duke and senators of Venice greet you.
    [Gives him a letter.]

OTHELLO
I kiss the instrument of their pleasures.
    [Opens the letter and reads.]

DESDEMONA
And what's the news, good cousin Lodovico?

IAGO
I am very glad to see you, signior.
Welcome to Cyprus.

LODOVICO
I thank you. How does Lieutenant Cassio?

IAGO   Lives, sir.

DESDEMONA
Cousin, there's fall'n between him and my lord
An unkind breach; but you shall make all well.

OTHELLO Are you sure of that?   220

---

206 *be his undertaker* undertake to deal with him

DESDEMONA My lord ?
OTHELLO *[reads]* 'This fail you not to do, as you will –'
LODOVICO
He did not call ; he's busy in the paper.
Is there division 'twixt thy lord and Cassio ?
DESDEMONA
A most unhappy one. I would do much
226   T' atone them, for the love I bear to Cassio.
OTHELLO
Fire and brimstone !
DESDEMONA   My lord ?
OTHELLO   Are you wise ?
DESDEMONA
What, is he angry ?
LODOVICO   May be the letter moved him ;
For, as I think, they do command him home,
Deputing Cassio in his government.
DESDEMONA
By my troth, I am glad on't.
OTHELLO   Indeed ?
DESDEMONA   My lord ?
OTHELLO
232   I am glad to see you mad.
DESDEMONA   Why, sweet Othello –
OTHELLO Devil !
        [Strikes her.]
DESDEMONA I have not deserved this.
LODOVICO
My lord, this would not be believed in Venice,
Though I should swear I saw't. 'Tis very much.
Make her amends ; she weeps.
OTHELLO   O devil, devil !
238   If that the earth could teem with woman's tears,
239   Each drop she falls would prove a crocodile.

226 *atone* reconcile 232 *mad* i.e. waggish 238 *teem* breed 239 *crocodile*
(crocodiles were supposed to shed hypocritical tears to lure men to destruction)

Out of my sight!

DESDEMONA   I will not stay to offend you.   *[Going.]*

LODOVICO

  Truly, an obedient lady.
  I do beseech your lordship call her back.

OTHELLO

  Mistress!

DESDEMONA My lord?

OTHELLO   What would you with her, sir?

LODOVICO

  Who? I, my lord?

OTHELLO

  Ay! You did wish that I would make her turn.
  Sir, she can turn, and turn, and yet go on
  And turn again; and she can weep, sir, weep;
  And she's obedient; as you say, obedient,
  Very obedient. – Proceed you in your tears. –
  Concerning this, sir – O well-painted passion! –   250
  I am commanded home. – Get you away;
  I'll send for you anon. – Sir, I obey the mandate
  And will return to Venice. – Hence, avaunt!
                                            [Exit Desdemona.]
  Cassio shall have my place. And, sir, to-night
  I do entreat that we may sup together.
  You are welcome, sir, to Cyprus. – Goats and monkeys!
                                                        Exit.

LODOVICO

  Is this the noble Moor whom our full Senate
  Call all in all sufficient? Is this the nature
  Whom passion could not shake? whose solid virtue
  The shot of accident nor dart of chance
  Could neither graze nor pierce?

IAGO   He is much changed.

LODOVICO

  Are his wits safe? Is he not light of brain?

250 *passion* grief

IAGO
> He's that he is; I may not breathe my censure.
> What he might be – if what he might he is not –
> I would to heaven he were!

LODOVICO   What, strike his wife?

IAGO
> Faith, that was not so well; yet would I knew
> That stroke would prove the worst!

267 LODOVICO   Is it his use?
> Or did the letters work upon his blood
> And new-create this fault?

IAGO   Alas, alas!
> It is not honesty in me to speak
> What I have seen and known. You shall observe him,
> And his own courses will denote him so
> That I may save my speech. Do but go after
> And mark how he continues.

LODOVICO
> I am sorry that I am deceived in him.   *Exeunt.*

*

IV, ii   *Enter Othello and Emilia.*

OTHELLO
> You have seen nothing then?

EMILIA
> Nor ever heard, nor ever did suspect.

OTHELLO
> Yes, you have seen Cassio and she together.

EMILIA
> But then I saw no harm, and then I heard
> Each syllable that breath made up between them.

OTHELLO
> What, did they never whisper?

EMILIA   Never, my lord.

267 *use* custom
IV, ii Within the castle

OTHELLO
Nor send you out o' th' way?
EMILIA Never.
OTHELLO
To fetch her fan, her gloves, her mask, nor nothing?
EMILIA Never, my lord.
OTHELLO That's strange.
EMILIA
I durst, my lord, to wager she is honest,
Lay down my soul at stake. If you think other,
Remove your thought; it doth abuse your bosom.   14
If any wretch have put this in your head,
Let heaven requite it with the serpent's curse!   16
For if she be not honest, chaste, and true,
There's no man happy; the purest of their wives
Is foul as slander.
OTHELLO   Bid her come hither. Go. *Exit Emilia.*
She says enough; yet she's a simple bawd
That cannot say as much. This is a subtle whore,
A closet lock and key of villainous secrets;
And yet she'll kneel and pray; I have seen her do't.
          Enter Desdemona and Emilia.
DESDEMONA
My lord, what is your will?
OTHELLO   Pray, chuck, come hither.
DESDEMONA
What is your pleasure?
OTHELLO   Let me see your eyes.
Look in my face.
DESDEMONA   What horrible fancy's this?
OTHELLO *[to Emilia]*
Some of your function, mistress.
Leave procreants alone and shut the door;   28
Cough or cry hem if anybody come.

14 *abuse . . . bosom* deceive your heart   16 *serpent's curse* (cf. Genesis iii, 14)
28 *procreants* mating couples

30   Your mystery, your mystery! Nay, dispatch!

Exit Emilia.

DESDEMONA
Upon my knees, what doth your speech import?
I understand a fury in your words,
[But not the words.]

OTHELLO
Why, what art thou?

DESDEMONA   Your wife, my lord; your true
And loyal wife.

OTHELLO   Come, swear it, damn thyself;
36   Lest, being like one of heaven, the devils themselves
Should fear to seize thee. Therefore be double-damned –
38   Swear thou art honest.

DESDEMONA   Heaven doth truly know it.

OTHELLO
Heaven truly knows that thou art false as hell.

DESDEMONA
To whom, my lord? With whom? How am I false?

OTHELLO
Ah, Desdemon! away! away! away!

DESDEMONA
Alas the heavy day! Why do you weep?
Am I the motive of these tears, my lord?
If haply you my father do suspect
45   An instrument of this your calling back,
Lay not your blame on me. If you have lost him,
Why, I have lost him too.

OTHELLO   Had it pleased heaven
To try me with affliction, had they rained
All kinds of sores and shames on my bare head,
Steeped me in poverty to the very lips,
Given to captivity me and my utmost hopes,
I should have found in some place of my soul

---

30 *mystery* trade, occupation   36 *being . . . heaven* looking like an angel
38 *honest* chaste   45 *An instrument* to be the cause

A drop of patience. But, alas, to make me
A fixèd figure for the time of scorn   54
To point his slow unmoving finger at !
Yet could I bear that too ; well, very well.
But there where I have garnered up my heart,
Where either I must live or bear no life,
The fountain from the which my current runs
Or else dries up – to be discarded thence,
Or keep it as a cistern for foul toads
To knot and gender in – turn thy complexion there,   62
Patience, thou young and rose-lipped cherubin !
Ay, there look grim as hell !

DESDEMONA
I hope my noble lord esteems me honest.

OTHELLO
O, ay ; as summer flies are in the shambles,   66
That quicken even with blowing. O thou weed,   67
Who art so lovely fair, and smell'st so sweet,
That the sense aches at thee, would thou hadst ne'er
    been born !

DESDEMONA
Alas, what ignorant sin have I committed ?

OTHELLO
Was this fair paper, this most goodly book,
Made to write 'whore' upon ? What committed ?
Committed ? O thou public commoner !   73
I should make very forges of my cheeks
That would to cinders burn up modesty,
Did I but speak thy deeds. What committed ?
Heaven stops the nose at it, and the moon winks ;   77
The bawdy wind, that kisses all it meets,
Is hushed within the hollow mine of earth
And will not hear it. What committed ?
Impudent strumpet !

54 *time of scorn* scornful world   62 *turn thy complexion there* change thy
color at that point   66 *shambles* slaughterhouse   67 *quicken* come to life
73 *commoner* harlot   77 *winks* closes her eyes

DESDEMONA   By heaven, you do me wrong!
OTHELLO
Are not you a strumpet?
DESDEMONA   No, as I am a Christian!
If to preserve this vessel for my lord
From any other foul unlawful touch
Be not to be a strumpet, I am none.
OTHELLO
What, not a whore?
DESDEMONA   No, as I shall be saved!
OTHELLO Is't possible?
DESDEMONA
O, heaven forgive us!
88 OTHELLO   I cry you mercy then.
I took you for that cunning whore of Venice
That married with Othello. – *[calling]* You, mistress,
That have the office opposite to Saint Peter
And keep the gate of hell!
          Enter Emilia.   You, you, ay, you!
We have done our course; there's money for your pains:
I pray you turn the key, and keep our counsel.   *Exit.*
EMILIA
Alas, what does this gentleman conceive?
How do you, madam? How do you, my good lady?
97 DESDEMONA Faith, half asleep.
EMILIA
Good madam, what's the matter with my lord?
DESDEMONA With who?
EMILIA Why, with my lord, madam.
DESDEMONA
Who is thy lord?
EMILIA   He that is yours, sweet lady.
DESDEMONA
I have none. Do not talk to me, Emilia.
I cannot weep; nor answers have I none

88 *cry you mercy* beg your pardon   97 *half asleep* i.e. stunned

But what should go by water. Prithee to-night
Lay on my bed my wedding sheets, remember;
And call thy husband hither.

EMILIA   Here's a change indeed! *Exit*.

DESDEMONA
'Tis meet I should be used so, very meet.
How have I been behaved, that he might stick
The small'st opinion on my least misuse?   109
        Enter Iago and Emilia.

IAGO
What is your pleasure, madam? How is't with you?

DESDEMONA
I cannot tell. Those that do teach young babes
Do it with gentle means and easy tasks:
He might have chid me so; for, in good faith,
I am a child to chiding.

IAGO   What is the matter, lady?

EMILIA
Alas, Iago, my lord hath so bewhored her,
Thrown such despite and heavy terms upon her
As true hearts cannot bear.

DESDEMONA
Am I that name, Iago?

IAGO   What name, fair lady?

DESDEMONA
Such as she said my lord did say I was.

EMILIA
He called her whore. A beggar in his drink
Could not have laid such terms upon his callet.   121

IAGO
Why did he so?

DESDEMONA
I do not know; I am sure I am none such.

IAGO
Do not weep, do not weep. Alas the day!

109 *small'st opinion* least suspicion; *least misuse* slightest misconduct   121
callet whore

EMILIA
Hath she forsook so many noble matches,
Her father and her country, and her friends,
To be called whore? Would it not make one weep?

DESDEMONA
It is my wretched fortune.

IAGO   Beshrew him for't!
129   How comes this trick upon him?

DESDEMONA   Nay, heaven doth know.

EMILIA
I will be hanged if some eternal villain,
Some busy and insinuating rogue,
132   Some cogging, cozening slave, to get some office,
Have not devised this slander. I'll be hanged else.

IAGO
Fie, there is no such man! It is impossible.

DESDEMONA
If any such there be, heaven pardon him!

EMILIA
A halter pardon him! and hell gnaw his bones!
Why should he call her whore? Who keeps her
company?
What place? what time? what form? what likelihood?
The Moor's abused by some most villainous knave,
Some base notorious knave, some scurvy fellow.
141   O heaven, that such companions thou'dst unfold,
And put in every honest hand a whip
To lash the rascals naked through the world
Even from the east to th' west!

144 **IAGO**   Speak within door.

EMILIA
O, fie upon them! Some such squire he was
That turned your wit the seamy side without
And made you to suspect me with the Moor.

---

129 *trick* freakish behavior   132 *cogging, cozening* cheating, defrauding
141 *companions* rogues; *unfold* expose   144 *within door* with restraint

IAGO
  You are a fool. Go to.
DESDEMONA   Alas, Iago,
  What shall I do to win my lord again?
  Good friend, go to him; for, by this light of heaven,
  I know not how I lost him. Here I kneel:
  If e'er my will did trespass 'gainst his love
  Either in discourse of thought or actual deed,   153
  Or that mine eyes, mine ears, or any sense
  Delighted them in any other form,
  Or that I do not yet, and ever did,
  And ever will (though he do shake me off
  To beggarly divorcement) love him dearly,
  Comfort forswear me! Unkindness may do much;   159
  And his unkindness may defeat my life,   160
  But never taint my love. I cannot say 'whore.'
  It does abhor me now I speak the word;
  To do the act that might the addition earn
  Not the world's mass of vanity could make me.
IAGO
  I pray you be content. 'Tis but his humor.
  The business of the state does him offense,
  [And he does chide with you.]
DESDEMONA
  If 'twere no other—
IAGO   'Tis but so, I warrant.
      [Trumpets within.]
  Hark how these instruments summon you to supper.
  The messengers of Venice stay the meat:
  Go in, and weep not. All things shall be well.
                          Exeunt Desdemona and Emilia.
      Enter Roderigo.
  How now, Roderigo?
RODERIGO I do not find that thou deal'st justly with me.

153 *discourse* course   159 *Comfort forswear* happiness forsake   160 *defeat*
destroy

IAGO What in the contrary?

175 RODERIGO Every day thou daff'st me with some device, Iago, and rather, as it seems to me now, keep'st from me

177 all conveniency than suppliest me with the least advantage of hope. I will indeed no longer endure it; nor am I yet persuaded to put up in peace what already I have foolishly suffered.

IAGO Will you hear me, Roderigo?

RODERIGO Faith, I have heard too much; for your words and performances are no kin together.

IAGO You charge me most unjustly.

RODERIGO With naught but truth. I have wasted myself out of my means. The jewels you have had from me to deliver to Desdemona would half have corrupted a

188 votarist. You have told me she hath received them, and

189 returned me expectations and comforts of sudden respect and acquaintance; but I find none.

IAGO Well, go to; very well.

RODERIGO Very well! go to! I cannot go to, man; nor 'tis not very well. By this hand, I say 'tis very scurvy,

194 and begin to find myself fopped in it.

IAGO Very well.

RODERIGO I tell you 'tis not very well. I will make myself known to Desdemona. If she will return me my jewels, I will give over my suit and repent my unlawful solicitation; if not, assure yourself I will seek satisfaction of you.

IAGO You have said now.

RODERIGO Ay, and said nothing but what I protest intendment of doing.

IAGO Why, now I see there's mettle in thee; and even from this instant do build on thee a better opinion than ever before. Give me thy hand, Roderigo. Thou hast taken against me a most just exception; but yet I protest

---

175 *thou . . . device* you put me off with some trick 177 *conveniency* favorable opportunities 188 *votarist* nun 189 *sudden respect* immediate notice 194 *fopped* duped

I have dealt most directly in thy affair.   207

RODERIGO It hath not appeared.

IAGO I grant indeed it hath not appeared, and your suspicion is not without wit and judgment. But, Roderigo, if
thou hast that in thee indeed which I have greater reason
to believe now than ever, I mean purpose, courage, and
valor, this night show it. If thou the next night following
enjoy not Desdemona, take me from this world with
treachery and devise engines for my life.   215

RODERIGO Well, what is it? Is it within reason and compass?

IAGO Sir, there is especial commission come from Venice
to depute Cassio in Othello's place.

RODERIGO Is that true? Why, then Othello and Desdemona return again to Venice.

IAGO O, no; he goes into Mauritania and takes away with
him the fair Desdemona, unless his abode be lingered   222
here by some accident; wherein none can be so deter-   223
minate as the removing of Cassio.

RODERIGO How do you mean removing of him?

IAGO Why, by making him uncapable of Othello's place –
knocking out his brains.

RODERIGO And that you would have me to do?

IAGO Ay, if you dare do yourself a profit and a right. He
sups to-night with a harlotry, and thither will I go to
him. He knows not yet of his honorable fortune. If you
will watch his going thence, which I will fashion to fall
out between twelve and one, you may take him at your
pleasure. I will be near to second your attempt, and he
shall fall between us. Come, stand not amazed at it, but
go along with me. I will show you such a necessity in his
death that you shall think yourself bound to put it on
him. It is now high supper time, and the night grows to
waste. About it!

---

207 *directly* straightforwardly   **215** *engines for* plots against   **222-23** *abode
. . . here* stay here be extended   **223** *determinate* effective

RODERIGO I will hear further reason for this.
IAGO And you shall be satisfied.   *Exeunt.*

*

IV, iii   *Enter Othello, Lodovico, Desdemona, Emilia, and*
              Attendants.

LODOVICO
  I do beseech you, sir, trouble yourself no further.
OTHELLO
  O, pardon me; 'twill do me good to walk.
LODOVICO
  Madam, good night. I humbly thank your ladyship.
DESDEMONA
  Your honor is most welcome.
OTHELLO   Will you walk, sir?
  O, Desdemona —
DESDEMONA My lord?
OTHELLO Get you to bed on th' instant; I will be re-
  turned forthwith. Dismiss your attendant there. Look't
  be done.
DESDEMONA I will, my lord.
                  Exit [Othello, with Lodovico and Attendants].
EMILIA How goes it now? He looks gentler than he did.
DESDEMONA
11 He says he will return incontinent.
  He hath commanded me to go to bed,
  And bade me to dismiss you.
EMILIA   Dismiss me?
DESDEMONA
  It was his bidding; therefore, good Emilia,
  Give me my nightly wearing, and adieu.
  We must not now displease him.
EMILIA I would you had never seen him!

IV, iii Within the castle 11 *incontinent* at once

DESDEMONA

So would not I. My love doth so approve him
That even his stubbornness, his checks, his frowns –   19
Prithee unpin me – have grace and favor in them.

EMILIA I have laid those sheets you bade me on the bed.

DESDEMONA

All's one. Good faith, how foolish are our minds!
If I do die before thee, prithee shroud me
In one of those same sheets.

EMILIA   Come, come! You talk.

DESDEMONA

My mother had a maid called Barbary.
She was in love; and he she loved proved mad   26
And did forsake her. She had a song of 'Willow';
An old thing 'twas; but it expressed her fortune,
And she died singing it. That song to-night
Will not go from my mind; I have much to do
But to go hang my head all at one side
And sing it like poor Barbary. Prithee dispatch.

EMILIA

Shall I go fetch your nightgown?   33

DESDEMONA   No, unpin me here.

This Lodovico is a proper man.

EMILIA A very handsome man.

DESDEMONA He speaks well.

EMILIA I know a lady in Venice would have walked barefoot to Palestine for a touch of his nether lip.

DESDEMONA *(sings)*

'The poor soul sat sighing by a sycamore tree,
    Sing all a green willow;
Her hand on her bosom, her head on her knee,
    Sing willow, willow, willow.
The fresh streams ran by her and murmured her
        moans;

---

19 *stubbornness* roughness; *checks* rebukes 26 *mad* wild, faithless 33
nightgown dressing gown

    Sing willow, willow, willow ;
  Her salt tears fell from her, and soft'ned the stones' –
Lay by these.
    'Sing willow, willow, willow' –
48 Prithee hie thee ; he'll come anon.
  'Sing all a green willow must be my garland.
  Let nobody blame him ; his scorn I approve' –
Nay, that's not next. Hark ! who is't that knocks ?

EMILIA It's the wind.

DESDEMONA *[sings]*
  'I called my love false love ; but what said he then ?
    Sing willow, willow, willow :
  If I court moe women, you'll couch with moe men.'
So, get thee gone ; good night. Mine eyes do itch.
Doth that bode weeping ?

EMILIA   'Tis neither here nor there.

DESDEMONA
I have heard it said so. O, these men, these men !
Dost thou in conscience think – tell me, Emilia –
60 That there be women do abuse their husbands
In such gross kind ?

EMILIA   There be some such, no question.

DESDEMONA
Wouldst thou do such a deed for all the world ?

EMILIA
Why, would not you ?

DESDEMONA   No, by this heavenly light !

EMILIA
Nor I neither by this heavenly light.
I might do't as well i' th' dark.

DESDEMONA
Wouldst thou do such a deed for all the world ?

EMILIA The world 's a huge thing ; it is a great price for a
small vice.

48 *hie thee* hurry

DESDEMONA
In troth, I think thou wouldst not.

EMILIA In troth, I think I should; and undo't when I
had done it. Marry, I would not do such a thing for a
joint-ring, nor for measures of lawn, nor for gowns, 72
petticoats, nor caps, nor any petty exhibition; but, for 73
all the whole world – 'Ud's pity! who would not make
her husband a cuckold to make him a monarch? I
should venture purgatory for't.

DESDEMONA
Beshrew me if I would do such a wrong
For the whole world.

EMILIA Why, the wrong is but a wrong i' th' world; and
having the world for your labor, 'tis a wrong in your
own world, and you might quickly make it right.

DESDEMONA I do not think there is any such woman.

EMILIA Yes, a dozen; and as many to th' vantage as 83
would store the world they played for. 84
But I do think it is their husbands' faults
If wives do fall. Say that they slack their duties
And pour our treasures into foreign laps;
Or else break out in peevish jealousies, 88
Throwing restraint upon us; or say they strike us,
Or scant our former having in despite – 90
Why, we have galls; and though we have some grace, 91
Yet have we some revenge. Let husbands know
Their wives have sense like them. They see, and smell,
And have their palates both for sweet and sour,
As husbands have. What is it that they do
When they change us for others? Is it sport?
I think it is. And doth affection breed it?
I think it doth. Is't frailty that thus errs?
It is so too. And have not we affections,

72 *joint-ring* ring made in separable halves 73 *exhibition* gift 83 *to th'*
vantage besides 84 *store* populate 88 *peevish* senseless 90 *having*
allowance 91 *galls* spirits to resent

Desires for sport, and frailty, as men have?
Then let them use us well; else let them know,
The ills we do, their ills instruct us so.

DESDEMONA

103   Good night, good night. God me such usage send,
Not to pick bad from bad, but by bad mend!   *Exeunt.*

*

V, i   *Enter Iago and Roderigo.*

IAGO

1   Here, stand behind this bulk; straight will he come.
Wear thy good rapier bare, and put it home.
Quick, quick! Fear nothing; I'll be at thy elbow.
It makes us, or it mars us – think on that,
And fix most firm thy resolution.

RODERIGO

Be near at hand; I may miscarry in't.

IAGO

Here, at thy hand. Be bold, and take thy stand.
          [Stands aside.]

RODERIGO

I have no great devotion to the deed,
And yet he hath given me satisfying reasons.
'Tis but a man gone. Forth my sword! He dies!

IAGO

11   I have rubbed this young quat almost to the sense,
And he grows angry. Now whether he kill Cassio,
Or Cassio him, or each do kill the other,
Every way makes my gain. Live Roderigo,
He calls me to a restitution large

16   Of gold and jewels that I bobbed from him
As gifts to Desdemona.
It must not be. If Cassio do remain,

103 *usage* habits
V, i A street in Cyprus   1 *bulk* projecting shop-front   11 *quat* pimple;
sense quick   16 *bobbed* swindled

He hath a daily beauty in his life
That makes me ugly ; and besides, the Moor
May unfold me to him ; there stand I in much peril.
No, he must die. Be't so ! I hear him coming.
    Enter Cassio.

RODERIGO

I know his gait. 'Tis he. Villain, thou diest !
    [Makes a pass at Cassio.]

CASSIO

That thrust had been mine enemy indeed
But that my coat is better than thou know'st.   25
I will make proof of thine.
    [Draws, and wounds Roderigo.]

RODERIGO   O, I am slain !
    [Iago darts from concealment behind Cassio,
        wounds him in the leg, and exit.]

CASSIO

I am maimed for ever. Help, ho ! Murder ! murder !
    [Falls.]
    Enter Othello.

OTHELLO

The voice of Cassio. Iago keeps his word.

RODERIGO

O, villain that I am !

OTHELLO   It is even so.

CASSIO

O, help, ho ! light ! a surgeon !

OTHELLO

'Tis he. O brave Iago, honest and just,
That hast such noble sense of thy friend's wrong !
Thou teachest me. Minion, your dear lies dead,   33
And your unblest fate hies. Strumpet, I come.   34
Forth of my heart those charms, thine eyes, are blotted.
Thy bed, lust-stained, shall with lust's blood be spotted.
                       Exit Othello.

---

25 *coat* under-shirt of mail   33 *Minion* mistress   34 *hies* hurries on

Enter Lodovico and Gratiano.

CASSIO

37   What, ho? No watch? No passage? Murder! murder!

GRATIANO

  'Tis some mischance. The cry is very direful.

CASSIO O, help!

LODOVICO Hark!

RODERIGO O wretched villain!

LODOVICO

42   Two or three groan. It is a heavy night.

  These may be counterfeits. Let's think't unsafe

  To come in to the cry without more help.

RODERIGO

  Nobody come? Then shall I bleed to death.

LODOVICO Hark!

Enter Iago, with a light.

GRATIANO

  Here's one comes in his shirt, with light and weapons.

IAGO

48   Who's there? Whose noise is this that cries on murder?

LODOVICO

  We do not know.

IAGO   Did not you hear a cry?

CASSIO

  Here, here! For heaven's sake, help me!

IAGO   What's the matter?

GRATIANO

  This is Othello's ancient, as I take it.

LODOVICO

  The same indeed, a very valiant fellow.

IAGO

  What are you here that cry so grievously?

CASSIO

  Iago? O, I am spoiled, undone by villains!

  Give me some help.

37 *passage* passers-by   42 *heavy* cloudy, dark   48 *cries on* raises the cry of

IAGO
O me, lieutenant! What villains have done this?

CASSIO
I think that one of them is hereabout
And cannot make away.   58

IAGO   O treacherous villains!
[To Lodovico and Gratiano]
What are you there? Come in, and give some help.

RODERIGO
O, help me here!

CASSIO
That's one of them.

IAGO   O murd'rous slave! O villain!
[Stabs Roderigo.]

RODERIGO
O damned Iago! O inhuman dog!

IAGO
Kill men i' th' dark? – Where be these bloody thieves? –
How silent is this town! – Ho! murder! murder! –
What may you be? Are you of good or evil?

LODOVICO
As you shall prove us, praise us.

IAGO Signior Lodovico?

LODOVICO He, sir.

IAGO
I cry you mercy. Here's Cassio hurt by villains.

GRATIANO Cassio?

IAGO How is't, brother?

CASSIO
My leg is cut in two.

IAGO   Marry, heaven forbid!   72
Light, gentleman. I'll bind it with my shirt.
     Enter Bianca.

BIANCA
What is the matter, ho? Who is't that cried?

58 *make* get   72 *Marry* (from By Mary)

IAGO
Who is't that cried?

BIANCA
O my dear Cassio! my sweet Cassio!
O Cassio, Cassio, Cassio!

IAGO
O notable strumpet! – Cassio, may you suspect
Who they should be that have thus mangled you?

CASSIO No.

GRATIANO I am sorry to find you thus. I have been to
seek you.

IAGO
82 Lend me a garter. So. O for a chair
To bear him easily hence!

BIANCA
Alas, he faints! O Cassio, Cassio, Cassio!

IAGO
Gentlemen all, I do suspect this trash
To be a party in this injury. –
Patience awhile, good Cassio. – Come, come!
Lend me a light. Know we this face or no?
Alas, my friend and my dear countryman
Roderigo? No. – Yes, sure. – O heaven, Roderigo!

GRATIANO What, of Venice?

IAGO
Even he, sir. Did you know him?

GRATIANO   Know him? Ay.

IAGO
Signior Gratiano? I cry your gentle pardon.
These bloody accidents must excuse my manners
That so neglected you.

GRATIANO   I am glad to see you.

IAGO
How do you, Cassio? – O, a chair, a chair!

GRATIANO Roderigo?

82 *chair* litter

IAGO

  He, he, 'tis he!

    [A chair brought in.] O, that's well said; the chair.   98

  Some good man bear him carefully from hence.

  I'll fetch the general's surgeon.

    [To Bianca]   For you, mistress,

  Save you your labor. – He that lies slain here, Cassio,

  Was my dear friend. What malice was between you?

CASSIO

  None in the world; nor do I know the man.

IAGO *[to Bianca]*

  What, look you pale? – O, bear him out o' th' air.

    [Cassio and Roderigo are borne off.]

  Stay you, good gentlemen. – Look you pale, mistress? –

  Do you perceive the gastness of her eye? –   106

  Nay, if you stare, we shall hear more anon.

  Behold her well; I pray you look upon her.

  Do you see, gentlemen? Nay, guiltiness will speak,

  Though tongues were out of use.

    Enter Emilia.

EMILIA

  'Las, what's the matter? What's the matter, husband?

IAGO

  Cassio hath here been set on in the dark

  By Roderigo, and fellows that are scaped.

  He's almost slain, and Roderigo dead.

EMILIA

  Alas, good gentleman! alas, good Cassio!

IAGO

  This is the fruits of whoring. Prithee, Emilia,

  Go know of Cassio where he supped to-night.

    [To Bianca]

  What, do you shake at that?

BIANCA

  He supped at my house; but I therefore shake not.

98 *well said* well done   106 *gastness* terror

IAGO
O, did he so? I charge you go with me.

EMILIA
Fie, fie upon thee, strumpet!

BIANCA
122   I am no strumpet, but of life as honest
As you that thus abuse me.

EMILIA   As I? Foh! fie upon thee!

IAGO
Kind gentlemen, let's go see poor Cassio dressed.
  [To Bianca]
Come, mistress, you must tell's another tale.
Emilia, run you to the citadel
And tell my lord and lady what hath happed.
                                          [Exit Emilia.]
Will you go on afore?   *Exeunt [all but Iago].*
                      This is the night
129   That either makes me or fordoes me quite.   *[Exit.]*

*

V, ii   *Desdemona [asleep] in her bed. Enter Othello with a*
             light.

OTHELLO
1   It is the cause, it is the cause, my soul.
Let me not name it to you, you chaste stars!
It is the cause. Yet I'll not shed her blood,
Nor scar that whiter skin of hers than snow,
And smooth as monumental alabaster.
Yet she must die, else she'll betray more men.
Put out the light, and then put out the light.
8   If I quench thee, thou flaming minister,
I can again thy former light restore,
Should I repent me; but once put out thy light,

122 *honest* chaste   129 *fordoes* destroys
V, ii A bedchamber in the castle   1 *cause* cause of justice   8 *minister*
servant

Thou cunning'st pattern of excelling nature,
I know not where is that Promethean heat   12
That can thy light relume. When I have plucked the rose,   13
I cannot give it vital growth again;
It needs must wither. I'll smell thee on the tree.
    He kisses her.
O balmy breath, that dost almost persuade
Justice to break her sword! One more, one more!
Be thus when thou art dead, and I will kill thee,
And love thee after. One more, and that's the last!
So sweet was ne'er so fatal. I must weep,
But they are cruel tears. This sorrow's heavenly;
It strikes where it doth love. She wakes.

DESDEMONA
Who's there? Othello?

OTHELLO   Ay, Desdemona.

DESDEMONA
Will you come to bed, my lord?

OTHELLO
Have you prayed to-night, Desdemon?

DESDEMONA   Ay, my lord.

OTHELLO
If you bethink yourself of any crime   26
Unreconciled as yet to heaven and grace,
Solicit for it straight.

DESDEMONA
Alack, my lord, what may you mean by that?

OTHELLO
Well, do it, and be brief; I will walk by.
I would not kill thy unprepared spirit.
No, heaven forfend! I would not kill thy soul.   32

DESDEMONA
Talk you of killing?

OTHELLO   Ay, I do.

DESDEMONA   Then heaven

---

12 *Promethean heat* divine fire   **13** *relume* relight   **26** *crime* sin   **32** *forfend* forbid

Have mercy on me!

OTHELLO   Amen, with all my heart!

DESDEMONA
If you say so, I hope you will not kill me.

OTHELLO Hum!

DESDEMONA
And yet I fear you; for you're fatal then
When your eyes roll so. Why I should fear I know not,
Since guiltiness I know not; but yet I feel I fear.

OTHELLO
Think on thy sins.

DESDEMONA   They are loves I bear to you.

OTHELLO
Ay, and for that thou diest.

DESDEMONA
That death's unnatural that kills for loving.
Alas, why gnaw you so your nether lip?
Some bloody passion shakes your very frame.
45   These are portents; but yet I hope, I hope,
They do not point on me.

OTHELLO   Peace and be still!

DESDEMONA
I will so. What's the matter?

OTHELLO
That handkerchief which I so loved and gave thee
Thou gav'st to Cassio.

DESDEMONA   No, by my life and soul!
Send for the man and ask him.

OTHELLO   Sweet soul, take heed,
Take heed of perjury; thou art on thy deathbed.

DESDEMONA
Ay, but not yet to die.

52 OTHELLO   Yes, presently.
Therefore confess thee freely of thy sin;
For to deny each article with oath

---

45 *portents* signs of impending violence   **52** *presently* at once

Cannot remove nor choke the strong conception   55
That I do groan withal. Thou art to die.

DESDEMONA
Then Lord have mercy on me!

OTHELLO   I say amen.

DESDEMONA
And have you mercy too! I never did
Offend you in my life; never loved Cassio   59
But with such general warranty of heaven
As I might love. I never gave him token.

OTHELLO
By heaven, I saw my handkerchief in's hand!
O perjured woman! thou dost stone my heart,   63
And mak'st me call what I intend to do
A murder, which I thought a sacrifice.
I saw the handkerchief.

DESDEMONA   He found it then.
I never gave it him. Send for him hither.
Let him confess a truth.

OTHELLO   He hath confessed.

DESDEMONA
What, my lord?

OTHELLO
That he hath used thee.

DESDEMONA   How? unlawfully?

OTHELLO   Ay.

DESDEMONA
He will not say so.

OTHELLO   No, his mouth is stopped.
Honest Iago hath ta'en order for't.   72

DESDEMONA
O, my fear interprets. What, is he dead?

OTHELLO
Had all his hairs been lives, my great revenge
Had stomach for them all.

---

55 *conception* belief   59 *Offend* wrong   63 *stone my heart* turn my heart to
stone   72 *ta'en order* taken measures

DESDEMONA
Alas, he is betrayed, and I undone!
OTHELLO
Out, strumpet! Weep'st thou for him to my face?
DESDEMONA
O, banish me, my lord, but kill me not!
OTHELLO
Down, strumpet!
DESDEMONA
80   Kill me to-morrow; let me live to-night!
OTHELLO
Nay, if you strive –
DESDEMONA
But half an hour!
OTHELLO   Being done, there is no pause.
DESDEMONA
But while I say one prayer!
OTHELLO   It is too late.
        Smothers her.
[DESDEMONA O Lord, Lord, Lord!]
        Emilia at the door.
EMILIA *(calls within)*
My lord, my lord! What, ho! my lord, my lord!
OTHELLO
What noise is this? Not dead? not yet quite dead?
I that am cruel am yet merciful;
I would not have thee linger in thy pain.
So, so.
EMILIA *(within)*
What, ho! my lord, my lord!
OTHELLO   Who's there?
EMILIA *[within]*
O, good my lord, I would speak a word with you!
OTHELLO
92   Yes, 'tis Emilia. – By and by. – She's dead. –

92 *By and by* just a moment (addressed to Emilia)

'Tis like she comes to speak of Cassio's death.
The noise was here. Ha! no more moving?
Still as the grave. – Shall she come in? Were't good? –
I think she stirs again. No. – What's best to do?
If she come in, she'll sure speak to my wife.
My wife! my wife! what wife? I have no wife.
O, insupportable! O heavy hour!
Methinks it should be now a huge eclipse
Of sun and moon, and that th' affrighted globe
Should yawn at alteration.   102

EMILIA *[within]*   I do beseech you
That I may speak with you, O good my lord!

OTHELLO
I had forgot thee. O, come in, Emilia.
Soft, by and by. – Let me the curtains draw. –
    [Closes the bed-curtains.]
Where art thou?
    [Opens the door.]
    Enter Emilia.
                      What's the matter with thee now?

EMILIA
O my good lord, yonder's foul murder done!

OTHELLO What? Now?

EMILIA But now, my lord.

OTHELLO
It is the very error of the moon.   110
She comes more nearer earth than she was wont
And makes men mad.

EMILIA
Cassio, my lord, hath killed a young Venetian
Called Roderigo.

OTHELLO   Roderigo killed?
And Cassio killed?

EMILIA   No, Cassio is not killed.

---

102 *yawn* open, as in an earthquake   110 *error* straying off course

OTHELLO
    Not Cassio killed? Then murder's out of tune,
    And sweet revenge grows harsh.

DESDEMONA
    O, falsely, falsely murdered!

EMILIA   O Lord! what cry is that?

OTHELLO That? What?

EMILIA
    Out and alas! that was my lady's voice.
    Help! help, ho! help! O lady, speak again!
    Sweet Desdemona! O sweet mistress, speak!

DESDEMONA
    A guiltless death I die.

EMILIA
    O, who hath done this deed?

DESDEMONA
    Nobody – I myself. Farewell.
126 Commend me to my kind lord. O, farewell!
            She dies.

OTHELLO
    Why, how should she be murd'red?

EMILIA   Alas, who knows?

OTHELLO
    You heard her say herself, it was not I.

EMILIA
    She said so. I must needs report the truth.

OTHELLO
    She's like a liar gone to burning hell!
    'Twas I that killed her.

EMILIA   O, the more angel she,
    And you the blacker devil!

OTHELLO
    She turned to folly, and she was a whore.

EMILIA
    Thou dost belie her, and thou art a devil.

126 *Commend* remember

OTHELLO
 She was false as water.   135
EMILIA   Thou art rash as fire to say
 That she was false. O, she was heavenly true !
OTHELLO
 Cassio did top her. Ask thy husband else.
 O, I were damned beneath all depth in hell
 But that I did proceed upon just grounds
 To this extremity. Thy husband knew it all.
EMILIA My husband ?
OTHELLO Thy husband.
EMILIA
 That she was false to wedlock ?
OTHELLO
 Ay, with Cassio. Nay, had she been true,
 If heaven would make me such another world
 Of one entire and perfect chrysolite,   146
 I'ld not have sold her for it.
EMILIA
 My husband ?
OTHELLO   Ay, 'twas he that told me first.
 An honest man he is, and hates the slime
 That sticks on filthy deeds.
EMILIA   My husband ?
OTHELLO
 What needs this iterance, woman ? I say thy husband. 151
EMILIA
 O mistress, villainy hath made mocks with love !
 My husband say that she was false ?
OTHELLO   He, woman.
 I say, thy husband. Dost understand the word ?
 My friend, thy husband ; honest, honest Iago.
EMILIA
 If he say so, may his pernicious soul
 Rot half a grain a day ! he lies to th' heart.

---

135 *water* (which is yielding) **146** *chrysolite* (precious topaz) **151** *iterance* repetition

She was too fond of her most filthy bargain.

OTHELLO Ha!

EMILIA Do thy worst.
This deed of thine is no more worthy heaven
Than thou wast worthy her.

OTHELLO   Peace, you were best.

EMILIA
Thou hast not half the power to do me harm
164 As I have to be hurt. O gull! O dolt!
As ignorant as dirt! thou hast done a deed –
I care not for thy sword; I'll make thee known,
Though I lost twenty lives. Help! help! Ho! help!
The Moor hath killed my mistress! Murder! murder!
        Enter Montano, Gratiano, Iago, and others.

MONTANO
What is the matter? How now, general?

EMILIA
170 O, are you come, Iago? You have done well,
That men must lay their murders on your neck.

GRATIANO
What is the matter?

EMILIA
Disprove this villain, if thou be'st a man.
He says thou told'st him that his wife was false.
I know thou didst not; thou'rt not such a villain.
Speak, for my heart is full.

IAGO
I told him what I thought, and told no more
Than what he found himself was apt and true.

EMILIA
But did you ever tell him she was false?

IAGO I did.

EMILIA
You told a lie, an odious damnèd lie!
Upon my soul, a lie! a wicked lie!

164 *to be hurt* to endure hurt

She false with Cassio ? Did you say with Cassio ?

IAGO
With Cassio, mistress. Go to, charm your tongue.   184

EMILIA
I will not charm my tongue ; I am bound to speak :
My mistress here lies murdered in her bed –

ALL
O heavens forfend !

EMILIA
And your reports have set the murder on.

OTHELLO
Nay, stare not, masters. It is true indeed.

GRATIANO
'Tis a strange truth.   190

MONTANO
O monstrous act !

EMILIA   Villainy, villainy, villainy !
I think upon't – I think I smell't ! – O villainy !
I thought so then. – I'll kill myself for grief. –
O villainy, villainy !

IAGO
What, are you mad ? I charge you get you home.

EMILIA
Good gentlemen, let me have leave to speak.
'Tis proper I obey him, but not now.
Perchance, Iago, I will ne'er go home.

OTHELLO
O ! O ! O !
          Falls on the bed.

EMILIA   Nay, lay thee down and roar !
For thou hast killed the sweetest innocent
That e'er did lift up eye.

OTHELLO   O, she was foul !
          [Rises.]
I scarce did know you, uncle. There lies your niece,

184 *charm* cast a spell on

147

Whose breath, indeed, these hands have newly stopped.
204 I know this act shows horrible and grim.

GRATIANO

Poor Desdemon! I am glad thy father's dead.
Thy match was mortal to him, and pure grief
Shore his old thread in twain. Did he live now,
208 This sight would make him do a desperate turn;
Yea, curse his better angel from his side,
210 And fall to reprobation.

OTHELLO

'Tis pitiful; but yet Iago knows
That she with Cassio hath the act of shame
A thousand times committed. Cassio confessed it;
214 And she did gratify his amorous works
215 With that recognizance and pledge of love
Which I first gave her. I saw it in his hand.
It was a handkerchief, an antique token
My father gave my mother.

EMILIA

O God! O heavenly God!

IAGO

Zounds, hold your peace!

EMILIA   'Twill out, 'twill out! I peace?
221 No, I will speak as liberal as the north.
Let heaven and men and devils, let them all,
All, all, cry shame against me, yet I'll speak.

IAGO

Be wise, and get you home.

EMILIA   I will not.
          [Iago draws and threatens Emilia.]
GRATIANO   Fie!
Your sword upon a woman?

EMILIA

O thou dull Moor, that handkerchief thou speak'st of

204 *shows* appears 208 *turn* act 210 *reprobation* rejection by God, damnation 214 *gratify* reward 215 *recognizance* token 221 *liberal as the north* unchecked as the north wind blows

I found by fortune, and did give my husband;
For often with a solemn earnestness —
More than indeed belonged to such a trifle —
He begged of me to steal't.

IAGO   Villainous whore!

EMILIA

She give it Cassio? No, alas, I found it,
And I did give't my husband.

IAGO   Filth, thou liest!

EMILIA

By heaven, I do not, I do not, gentlemen.
O murd'rous coxcomb! what should such a fool
Do with so good a wife?

OTHELLO   Are there no stones in heaven   235
But what serves for the thunder? Precious villain!

The Moor runs at Iago [but is disarmed by Montano].
Iago kills his wife.

GRATIANO

The woman falls. Sure he hath killed his wife.

EMILIA

Ay, ay. O, lay me by my mistress' side.   *Exit Iago.*

GRATIANO

He's gone, but his wife's killed.

MONTANO

'Tis a notorious villain. Take you this weapon,   240
Which I have here recovered from the Moor.
Come, guard the door without. Let him not pass,
But kill him rather. I'll after that same villain,
For 'tis a damnèd slave.

Exit [Montano, with all but Othello and Emilia].

OTHELLO   I am not valiant neither;
But every puny whipster gets my sword.   245
But why should honor outlive honesty?
Let it go all.

EMILIA   What did thy song bode, lady?

---

235 *stones* bolts like those used for thunderbolts   240 *notorious* notable
245 *puny whipster* top-whipping boy

Hark, canst thou hear me? I will play the swan,
And die in music. *[Sings]* 'Willow, willow, willow.'
Moor, she was chaste. She loved thee, cruel Moor:
So come my soul to bliss as I speak true.
So speaking as I think, alas, I die.
          She dies.

OTHELLO
I have another weapon in this chamber;
254   It is a sword of Spain, the ice brook's temper.
O, here it is. – Uncle, I must come forth.

GRATIANO *(within)*
If thou attempt it, it will cost thee dear.
Thou hast no weapon, and perforce must suffer.

OTHELLO
Look in upon me then and speak with me,
259   Or, naked as I am, I will assault thee.
          [Enter Gratiano.]

GRATIANO
What is the matter?

OTHELLO   Behold, I have a weapon;
A better never did itself sustain
Upon a soldier's thigh. I have seen the day
That with this little arm and this good sword
I have made my way through more impediments
265   Than twenty times your stop. But O vain boast!
Who can control his fate? 'Tis not so now.
Be not afraid, though you do see me weaponed.
268   Here is my journey's end, here is my butt,
269   And very seamark of my utmost sail:
270   Do you go back dismayed? 'Tis a lost fear.
271   Man but a rush against Othello's breast,
And he retires. Where should Othello go?
Now, how dost thou look now? O ill-starred wench!

---

254 *ice brook's* i.e. a Spanish blade, tempered in cold running water   259
naked disarmed   265 *stop* power to stop   268 *butt* limit   269 *seamark*
beacon, destination   270 *lost* wasted   271 *Man but a rush* wield only a reed

Pale as thy smock! When we shall meet at compt, 274
This look of thine will hurl my soul from heaven,
And fiends will snatch at it. Cold, cold, my girl?
Even like thy chastity.
O cursèd, cursèd slave! Whip me, ye devils,
From the possession of this heavenly sight!
Blow me about in winds! roast me in sulphur!
Wash me in steep-down gulfs of liquid fire!
Oh Desdemon! dead Desdemon! dead! Oh! Oh!
 Enter Lodovico, Montano, Iago [as prisoner,] and
 Officers; Cassio in a chair.

LODOVICO
Where is this rash and most unfortunate man?

OTHELLO
That's he that was Othello. Here I am.

LODOVICO
Where is that viper? Bring the villain forth.

OTHELLO
I look down towards his feet – but that's a fable. 286
If that thou be'st a devil, I cannot kill thee.
 [Wounds Iago.]

LODOVICO
Wrench his sword from him.
 [Othello is disarmed.]

IAGO   I bleed, sir, but not killed.

OTHELLO
I am not sorry neither. I'ld have thee live;
For in my sense, 'tis happiness to die.

LODOVICO
O thou Othello that wert once so good,
Fall'n in the practice of a damnèd slave, 292
What shall be said to thee?

OTHELLO   Why, anything:
An honorable murderer, if you will;
For naught did I in hate, but all in honor.

274 *compt* final accounting, Last Judgment   **286** *I . . . feet* i.e. to see if they
are cloven, like the Devil's   **292** *practice* plot

LODOVICO
      This wretch hath part confessed his villainy.
297   Did you and he consent in Cassio's death ?
OTHELLO Ay.
CASSIO
      Dear general, I never gave you cause.
OTHELLO
      I do believe it, and I ask your pardon.
      Will you, I pray, demand that demi-devil
      Why he hath thus ensnared my soul and body ?
IAGO
      Demand me nothing. What you know, you know.
      From this time forth I never will speak word.
LODOVICO
      What, not to pray ?
GRATIANO   Torments will ope your lips.
OTHELLO
      Well, thou dost best.
LODOVICO
      Sir, you shall understand what hath befall'n,
      Which, as I think, you know not. Here is a letter
      Found in the pocket of the slain Roderigo ;
310   And here another. The one of them imports
      The death of Cassio to be undertook
      By Roderigo.
OTHELLO
      O villain !
CASSIO   Most heathenish and most gross !
LODOVICO
      Now here's another discontented paper
      Found in his pocket too ; and this, it seems,
      Roderigo meant t' have sent this damnèd villain ;
317   But that, belike, Iago in the nick
      Came in and satisfied him.

OTHELLO   O thou pernicious caitiff! –
How came you, Cassio, by that handkerchief
That was my wife's?

CASSIO   I found it in my chamber;
And he himself confessed but even now
That there he dropped it for a special purpose
Which wrought to his desire.

OTHELLO   O fool! fool! fool!

CASSIO
There is besides in Roderigo's letter,
How he upbraids Iago that he made him
Brave me upon the watch; whereon it came
That I was cast; and even but now he spake,   327
After long seeming dead – Iago hurt him,
Iago set him on.

LODOVICO
You must forsake this room and go with us.
Your power and your command is taken off,
And Cassio rules in Cyprus. For this slave,
If there be any cunning cruelty
That can torment him much and hold him long,
It shall be his. You shall close prisoner rest
Till that the nature of your fault be known
To the Venetian state. Come, bring away.

OTHELLO
Soft you! a word or two before you go.
I have done the state some service, and they know't.
No more of that. I pray you, in your letters,
When you shall these unlucky deeds relate,   341
Speak of me as I am. Nothing extenuate,
Nor set down aught in malice. Then must you speak
Of one that loved not wisely, but too well;
Of one not easily jealous, but, being wrought,
Perplexed in the extreme; of one whose hand,   346

327 *cast* dismissed   341 *unlucky* fatal   346 *Perplexed* distracted

347 Like the base Judean, threw a pearl away
348 Richer than all his tribe; of one whose subdued eyes,
Albeit unusèd to the melting mood,
Drop tears as fast as the Arabian trees
Their med'cinable gum. Set you down this.
And say besides that in Aleppo once,
Where a malignant and a turbaned Turk
Beat a Venetian and traduced the state,
I took by th' throat the circumcisèd dog
And smote him – thus.
            He stabs himself.

LODOVICO
357 O bloody period!
GRATIANO   All that's spoke is marred.
OTHELLO
I kissed thee ere I killed thee. No way but this,
Killing myself, to die upon a kiss.
            He [falls upon the bed and] dies.

CASSIO
This did I fear, but thought he had no weapon;
For he was great of heart.
LODOVICO *[to Iago]*   O Spartan dog,
362 More fell than anguish, hunger, or the sea!
Look on the tragic loading of this bed.
This is thy work. The object poisons sight;
365 Let it be hid. Gratiano, keep the house,
366 And seize upon the fortunes of the Moor,
For they succeed on you. To you, lord governor,
368 Remains the censure of this hellish villain,
The time, the place, the torture. O, enforce it!
Myself will straight aboard, and to the state
This heavy act with heavy heart relate.   *Exeunt.*

---

347 *Judean* Judas Iscariot (?) (quarto reads 'Indian') 348 *subdued* i.e.
conquered by grief 357 *period* ending 362 *fell* cruel 365 *Let it be hid* i.e.
draw the bed curtains 366 *seize upon* take legal possession of 368 *censure*
judicial sentence

APPENDIX:
THE QUARTO AND FOLIO TEXTS

Listed below are all departures from the folio text (F) except for the correction of a few obvious typographical errors and the addition of the bracketed lines mentioned in the "Note on the text." The great majority of these departures represent readings in the quarto (Q), the copy for which may have been a transcript of Shakespeare's draft. Although not printed until 1622, the quarto text remains totally unaffected by the Parliamentary ruling against the use of oaths in stage plays theoretically in force since 1606. On the other hand the folio text, which appears to have derived from the quarto collated with a prompt-book, reveals an unusual scrupulousness in observing this ruling. Perhaps the chief interest in the following list of variants in quarto and folio is the indication of the great variety of expressions which the acting company feared might be considered "oaths." Also of interest is the list of substitutes found for them. The adopted reading in italics is followed by the folio reading in roman.

The Names of the Actors (printed at the end of the play in F)
I, i, 1 *Tush* (Q) Omitted 4 *'Sblood* (Q) Omitted 25 *togèd* (Q) Tongued 30 *Christian* (Q) Christen'd 33 *God* (Q) Omitted 66 *full* (Q) fall 72 *changes* (Q) chances 79 *Thieves! thieves! thieves!* (Q) Theeues, Theeues 81 s.d. *Brabantio at a window* (Q) Omitted 86 *Zounds* (Q) Omitted 103 *spirit* (Q) spirits *them* (Q) their 108 *Zounds* (Q) Omitted 116 *now* (Q) Omitted 122 *odd-even* (Malone) odde Euen 145 *produced* (Q) producted 150 *stand* (Pope) stands 153 *hell-pains* (Dyce) hell apines (F) hells paines (Q) 158 s.d. *and . . . with* (Q) with . . . and *in his nightgown* (Q) Omitted 181 *night* (Q) might 182 *I'll* (Q) I Will
I, ii, s.d. *and* (Q) Omitted 4 *Sometimes* (Q) Sometime 15 *and*

(Q) or   33 s.d. *Officers* (Q) Omitted   34 *Duke* (Q) Dukes   38
What's (Q) What is   54 s.d. *and others . . . weapons* (Q) with
Officers, and Torches   68 *darlings* (Q) Deareling   75 *weaken*
(Rowe) weakens   84 *Where* (Q) Whether

I, iii, s.d. *and Senators . . . Attendants* (Q) Senators, and Officers
1 *There is* (Q) There's   *these* (Q) this   87 *broil* (Q) Broiles   93
am I (Q) I am   106 *Duke* (Q) Omitted   107 *certain* (Q) wider
121 s.d. *Exit . . . two or three* (Q) Omitted   130 *fortunes* (Q)
Fortune   139 *travels'* (Q) Trauellours   141 *and* (Q) Omitted
142 *the* (Q) my   145 *Do grow* (Q) Grew   *This* (Q) These things
147 *thence* (Q) hence   155 *intentively* (Q) instinctiuely   159
sighs (Q) kisses   160 *i' faith* (Q) in faith   201 *Into your favor* (Q)
Omitted   219 *ear* (Q) eares   220 *Beseech you, now* (Q) I humbly
beseech you proceed   *the affairs* (Q) th' Affaires   230 *couch*
(Pope) Coach   234 *These* (Malone) This   239–40 *If you
please, | Be't at her father's.* (Q) Why at her Fathers?   241 *Nor
I. I would not* (Q) Nor would I   248 *did* (Q) Omitted   257
which (Q) why   263–64 *heat – the young affects | In me defunct –*
(Capell) heat the yong affects | In my defunct,   270 *instru-
ments* (Q) Instrument   293 s.d. *Exeunt* (Q) Exit   299 *matters*
(Q) matter   300 s.d. *Moor and Desdemona* (Q) Omitted   322
thyme (Pope) Time   326 *balance* (Q) braine   330 *our unbitted*
(Q) or vnbitted   340 *be that Desdemona should long continue* (Q)
be long that Desdemona should continue   348 *error* (Q) errors
355 *'Tis* (Q) it is   379 *a snipe* (Q) snpe   382 *H'as* (Q) She ha's
398 s.d. *Exit* (Q) Omitted

II, i, 13 *mane* (Knight) Maine   19 s.d. *third* (Q) Omitted   33 *prays*
(Q) praye   34 *heaven* (Q) Heauens   42 *arrivance* (Q) arrivancie
43 *this* (Q) the   50 *hopes* (F3) hope's   51 s.d. *Enter a Messenger*
(Q) Omitted   53 *Messenger* (Q) Gent.   55 s.d. *A shot* (Q) Omitted
65 *ingener* (Knight) Ingeniuer   s.d. *Second* (Q) Omitted   70
clog (Q) enclogge   88 *me* (Q) Omitted   92 *the sea* (Q) Sea   93
(Within) A sail, a sail! [A shot.] But hark. A sail! (Collier) But
hearke, a Saile. | *Within.* A Saile, a Saile.   94 *their* (Q) this   104
list (Q) leaue   117 *thou write* (Q) write   157 *such wight* (Q) such
wightes   168 *gyve* (F2) giue   173 *an* (Q) and   174 *courtesy* (Q)
curtsy   176 s.d. *Trumpet within* (Q2) Omitted   196 s.d. *They
kiss* (Q) Omitted   210 s.d. *Exit Othello* (Eds) Exit Othello and
Desdemona   212 *hither* (Q) thither   221–22 *and will she* (Q)
To   225 *again* (Q) a game   237 *compassing* (Q) compasse   239
finder-out (Q) finder   *occasions* (Q) occasion   *has* (Q) he's   255

mutualities (Q) mutabilities   267 *with his truncheon* (Q) Omitted
293 *for wife* (Q) wift   297 *I trash* (Steevens) I trace   300 *rank*
(Q) right

II, ii, 5 *addiction* (Q2) addition   10 *Heaven* (Q) Omitted

II, iii (Capell first begins a new scene here)   37 *unfortunate* (Q)
infortunate   51 *lads* (Q) else   56 *to put* (Q) put to   60 *God* (Q)
heauen   67 *A life's* (Q) Oh, mans life's   71 *God* (Q) Heauen   76
expert (Q) exquisite   84 *a* (Q) and-a   86 *'em* (Q) them   91 *Then*
(Q) And   *auld* (Q) awl'd   93 *'Fore God* (Q) Why   97 *God's* (Q)
heau'ns   106 *God* (Q) Omitted   131 s.d. *Exit Roderigo* (Q)
Omitted   138 *(Within) Help! help!* (Q) Omitted   s.d. *driving
in* (Q) pursuing   139 *Zounds* (Q) Omitted   145 s.d. *They fight*
(Q) Omitted   146 s.d. *Exit Roderigo* (Q2) Omitted   147 *God's
will* (Q2) Alas   148 *sir – Montano – sir –* (Capell) Sir Montano
(F) Sir, Montanio, sir (Q2)   149 s.d. *A bell rung* (Q) Omitted
151 *God's will, lieutenant, hold!* (Q) Fie, fie Lieutenant,   152
shamed (Q) asham'd   s.d. *and Gentlemen with weapons* (Q) and
Attendants   153 *Zounds* (Q) Omitted   156 *Hold, hold* (Q)
Hold hoa   *sir – Montano –* (Rowe) Sir Montano   157 *sense of
place* (Hanmer) place of sense   173 *breast* (Q) breastes   208
leagued (Pope) league   241 *What's* (Q2) What is   *matter* (Q)
matter (Deere?)   242 *now* (Q) Omitted   246 *vile* (Q) vil'd   251
God (Q) Heauen   256 *thought* (Q) had thought   261 *ways* (Q)
more wayes   277 *God* (Q) Omitted   281 *Why,* (Q) Why?   288
so (Q) Omitted   299 *some* (Q) a   300 *I'll* (Q) I   303 *denotement*
(Theobald) deuotement   316 *here* (Q) Omitted   326 *were't* (Q)
were   337 *fortunes* (Q) Fortune   357 *hast* (Q) hath   360 *By
the mass* (Q) Introth   366 *on;* (Q) on   367 *the while* (Theobald)
a while

III, i, 3 *ha'* (Q) haue   21 *hear, my* (Capell) heare me, mine (F) hear
my (Q)   25 *general's wife* (Q2) Generall   29 *Cassio. Do, good
my friend* (Q) Omitted   53 *Desdemona* (Q) Desdemon   55 s.d.
Exeunt (Q) Omitted

III, ii, 6 *We'll* (F3) well

III, iii, 16 *circumstance* (Q) circumstances   52 *Yes, faith* (Q) I
sooth   60 *or* (Q) on   61 *or Wednesday* (Q) on Wensday   63 *I'
faith* (Q) Infaith   65 *examples* (Q) example   66 *their* (Rowe) her
69 *could* (Q) would   74 *By'r Lady* (Q) Trust me   87 *Desdemon*
(Dyce iii) Desdemona   94 *you* (Q) he   106 *By heaven* (Q) Alas
he echoes (Q) thou ecchos't   107 *his* (Q) thy   112 *In* (Q) Of   135
that all (Q) that: All   *free to* (Q) free   136 *vile* (Q) vild   138 *a*

(Q) that   139 *But some* (Q) Wherein   147 *oft* (Q) of   148 *yet*
(Q2) Omitted   149 *conjects* (Q) conceits   162 *By heaven* (Q)
Omitted   170 *strongly* (Q) soundly   175 *God* (Q) Heauen   180
once (Q) Omitted   182 *blown* (Q) blow'd   202 *God* (Q) Heauen
204 *keep't* (Q) kept   215 *I' faith* (Q) Trust me   217 *my* (Q) your
222 *vile* (Q) vilde   223 *As* (Q) Which   *aim not at* (Q) aym'd not
248 *hold* (Q) Omitted   259 *qualities* (Q) Quantities   *learned* (Q)
learn'd   262 *I'd* (Q) I'ld   273 *of* (Q) to   278 *O, then* (Q) Omitted   *mocks* (Q) mock'd   285 *Faith* (Q) Why   302 *A thing* (Q)
You haue a thing   311 *No, faith ; she* (Q) No : but she   313 *it is*
(Q) 'tis   332 *med'cine* (Eds) medicine   338 *of her* (Q) in her
349 *troop* (Q) Troopes   375 *b' wi'* (F4) buy   376 *liv'st* (Eds)
lou'st (F) liuest (Q)   386 *Her* (Q2) My   391 *sir* (Q) Omitted
393 *I* (Q) and I   395 *supervisor* (Q) supervision   408 *may* (Q)
might   422 *and* (Q) Omitted   424 *then* (Q) Omitted   425
Over (Q) ore   *sighed* (Q) sigh   *kissed* (Eds) kisse (F) kissèd (Q)
426 *Cried* (Q) cry   432 *but* (Q) yet   440 *that was* (Malone) it
was   452 *perhaps* (Q) Omitted   455 *feels* (Q2) keepes   460
s.d. *He kneels* (Eds) Omitted (F) (in Rowe after l. 461, in Q after
l. 450)   462 s.d. *Iago kneels* (Q2) Omitted

III, iv, 5 *is* (Q) 'tis   22 *I'll* (Q) I will   *of* (Q) Omitted   s.d. *Exit*
(Q) Exit Clo.   23 *that* (Q) the   37 *yet* (Q) Omitted   48 *Come
now,* (Capell) Come, now   54 *faith* (Q) indeed   64 *wive* (Q)
wiu'd   73 *hallowed* (Capell) hallowèd   75 *I' faith* (Q) Indeed
77 *God* (Q) Heauen   80 *is it* (Q) is't   81 *Heaven* (Q) Omitted
86 *sir* (Q) Omitted   97 *I' faith* (Q) Insooth   98 *Zounds* (Q)
Away   116 *neither* (Q) nor my   161 *'Tis* (Q) It is   163 *that* (Q)
the   168 s.d. *Exeunt Desdemona and Emilia* (Q) Exit   171 *I'
faith* (Q) Indeed   182 *absence now* (Capell) Absence : now   184
vile (Q) vilde   187 *by my faith* (Q) in good troth   188 *sweet* (Q)
neither   190 *I'd* (Q) I would   201 s.d. *Exeunt* (Q) Exeunt
omnes

IV, i, 9 *So* (Q) If   21 *infected* (Q) infectious   32 *Faith* (Q) Why
36 *Zounds* (Q) Omitted   45 *med'cine* (Eds) Medicine   *work* (Q)
workes   52 *No, forbear* (Q) Omitted   60 *you? No* (Q) you not
77 *unsuiting* (Q) resulting   79 *'scuse* (Q) scuses   95 *clothes* (Q)
Cloath   98 *refrain* (Q) restraine   101 *conster* (Q) conserue   102
behavior (Q) behauiours   103 *now* (Q) Omitted   107 *power* (Q)
dowre   110 *a* (Q) Omitted   111 *i' faith* (Q) indeed   118 *you
triumph, Roman* (Q) ye triumph, Romaine   119 *her* (Q) Omitted
122 *win* (F4) winnes   123 *Faith* (Q) Why   *shall* (Q) Omitted

130 *beckons* (Q) becomes   133–34 *by this hand, she* (Q) Omitted
149 *whole* (Q) Omitted   157 *An . . . an* (Q) If . . . if   160 *Faith*
(Q) Omitted   *street* (Q) streets   166 s.d. *Exit Cassio* (Q) Omitted   189 *thousand thousand* (Q) thousand, a thousand   208 s.d.
A trumpet (Q) Omitted   210 *and* (Q) Omitted   *wife is* (Q) wife's
211 *God* (Q) Omitted   212 *senators* (Q) the Senators   224 *thy*
(Q) my   228 *the letter* (Q) th Letter   231 *By my troth* (Q) Trust
me   241 *an* (Q) Omitted   269 *this* (Q) his

IV, ii, 24 *Pray* (Q) Pray you   30 *Nay* (Q) May   31 *knees* (Q) knee
47 *Why* (Q) Omitted   54 *A* (Q) The   55 *unmoving* (Q) and
mouing   64 *Ay, there* (Theobald) I heere   69 *ne'er* (Q) neuer
71 *paper,* (Q) Paper ?   80 *hear it* (Steevens) hear't   81 *Impudent*
strumpet (Q) Omitted   92 *keep* (Rowe) keepes   117 *As* (Q)
That   *bear* (Q) beare it   133 *I'll* (Q) I will   141 *heaven* (Q)
heauens   155 *them in* (Q2) them : or   168 *'Tis* (Q) It is   169
you (Q) Omitted   170 *stay* (Q) staies   175 *daff'st* (Collier)
dafts   180 *suffered* (Q) suffred   182 *Faith* (Q) Omitted   *for* (Q)
and   187 *deliver to* (Q) deliuer   193 *By this hand, I say 'tis very*
(Q) Nay I think it is   221 *takes* (Q) taketh   222 *lingered* (Q)
lingred   225 *of* (Q) Omitted

IV, iii, 12 *He* (Q) And   13 *bade* (Q) bid   20 *in them* (Q) Omitted
22 *faith* (Q) Father   23 *thee* (Q) Omitted   24 *those* (Q) these
39 s.d. *sings* (Q2) Omitted   *sighing* (Q2) singing   46–47 *Lay . . .*
willow' (Eds) Sing Willough, &c. (Lay by these)   48–49 *Prithee*
. . . garland (Eds) Willough, Willough. (Prythee high thee : he'le
come anon)   71 *it* (Q) Omitted   74 *'Ud's pity* (Q) why   103
God (Q) Heauen   *usage* (Q) uses

V, i, 1 *bulk* (Q) Barke   22 *Be't* (Q) But   *hear* (Q) heard   35 *Forth*
(Q) For   38 *cry* (Q) voyce   42 *It is a* (Q) 'Tis   46 s.d. *with a*
light (Q) Omitted   49 *Did* (Q) Do   50 *heaven's* (Q) heauen   60
here (Q) there   90 *O heaven* (Q) Yes, 'tis   104 *out* (Q) Omitted
110 s.d. *Enter Emilia* (Q) Omitted   111 *'Las, what's . . . What's*
(Q) Alas, what is . . . What is   114 *dead* (Q) quite dead   121 *Fie,*
fie (Q) Oh fie   123 *Foh* (Q) Omitted

V, ii, s.d. *Desdemona [asleep] in her bed. Enter Othello with a light*
(Eds) Enter Othello, and Desdemona in her bed (F) Enter
Othello with a light, and Desdemona in her bed (Q2)   15 s.d.
He kisses her (Q, after ll. 19–20) Omitted (F) Kisses her (Q2)
32 *heaven* (Q) Heauens   35 *so* (Q) Omitted   41 *diest* (Q) dy'st
52 *Yes* (Q) Omitted   57 *Then Lord* (Q) O Heauen   64 *mak'st*
(Q2) makes   85 s.d. *calls within* (Q) Omitted   87 *that am* (Q) am

that 94 *here* (Q) high 102 *Should* (Q) Did 107 *murder*
(Theobald) murthers 118 *O Lord* (Q) Alas 126 s.d. *She dies*
(Q) Omitted 128 *heard* (Q) heare 144 *Nay* (Q) Omitted 148
me (Q) me on her 153 *that* (Q2) Omitted 163 *the* (Q) that
168 s.d. *Gratiano, Iago, and others* (Q) Gratiano, and Iago 186
murdered (Pope) murtherèd 199 s.d. *Falls on the bed* (Eds)
Omitted (F) Oth. fals on the bed (Q) 210 *reprobation* (Q) Re-
probance 219 *O God! O heavenly God* (Q) Oh Heauen! oh
heauenly Powres 220 *Zounds* (Q) Come 236 s.d. *The Moor
. . . wife* (Q) Omitted 238 s.d. *Exit Iago* (Q) Omitted 241 *here*
(Q) Omitted 252 s.d. *She dies* (Q) Omitted 254 *is* (Q) was
256 s.d. *within* (Q) Omitted 282 s.d. *Enter . . . chair* (Q) Enter
Lodouico, Cassio, Montano, and Iago, with Officers 291 *wert*
(Q) was 292 *damnèd* (Q) cursed 295 *did I* (Q) I did 317 *nick*
(Q) interim 321 *but* (Capell) it but 346 *Perplexed* (Q) Per-
plexèd 350 *Drop* (Q2) Drops 351 *med'cinable* (Capell) Medi-
cinable 356 s.d. *He stabs himself* (Q) Omitted 357 *that's* (Q)
that is 359 s.d. *He . . . dies* (Q) Dyes